D0016978

INTERNATIONAL

BOOKS BY EUDORA WELTY

A Curtain of Green
The Robber Bridegroom
The Wide Net
Delta Wedding
The Golden Apples
The Ponder Heart
The Bride of the Innisfallen
Losing Battles
One Time, One Place
The Eye of the Story
One Writer's Beginnings

The Optimist's Daughter

Eudora Welty

The Optimist's Daughter

Vintage International

Vintage Books

A Division of Random House, Inc.

New York

Vintage International Edition, August 1990

Copyright © 1969, 1972 by Eudora Welty

All rights reserved under International and Pan-American
Copyright Conventions. Published in the United States by
Vintage Books, a division of Random House, Inc., New York,
and in Canada by Random House of Canada Limited, Toronto.
Originally published by Random House, Inc., in May 1972.

The Optimist's Daughter appeared originally in *The New
Yorker* in a shorter and different form.

Library of Congress Cataloging in Publication Data
Welty, Eudora, 1909–
The optimist's daughter.
I. Title
PZ3.W6960p 1978   [PS3545.E6]   813'.5'2   89-40630
ISBN 0-679-72883-X

Manufactured in the United States of America
40 39 38 37 36 35

For C.A.W.

One

I

A NURSE held the door open for them. Judge McKelva going first, then his daughter Laurel, then his wife Fay, they walked into the windowless room where the doctor would make his examination. Judge McKelva was a tall, heavy man of seventy-one who customarily wore his glasses on a ribbon. Holding them in his hand now, he sat on the raised, thronelike chair above the doctor's stool, flanked by Laurel on one side and Fay on the other.

Laurel McKelva Hand was a slender, quiet-faced woman in her middle forties, her hair still dark. She wore clothes of an interesting cut and texture, although her suit was wintry for New Orleans and had a wrinkle down the skirt. Her dark blue eyes looked sleepless.

Fay, small and pale in her dress with the gold buttons, was tapping her sandaled foot.

It was a Monday morning of early March. New Orleans was out-of-town for all of them.

Dr. Courtland, on the dot, crossed the room in long steps and shook hands with Judge McKelva and Laurel. He had to be introduced to Fay, who had been married to Judge McKelva for only a year and a half. Then the doctor was on the stool, with his heels hung over the rung. He lifted his face in appreciative atten-

3

tion: as though it were he who had waited in New Orleans for Judge McKelva—in order to give the Judge a present, or for the Judge to bring him one.

"Nate," Laurel's father was saying, "the trouble may be I'm not as young as I used to be. But I'm ready to believe it's something wrong with my *eyes*."

As though he had all the time in the world, Dr. Courtland, the well-known eye specialist, folded his big country hands with the fingers that had always looked, to Laurel, as if their mere touch on the crystal of a watch would convey to their skin exactly what time it was.

"I date this little disturbance from George Washington's Birthday," Judge McKelva said.

Dr. Courtland nodded, as though that were a good day for it. "Tell me about the little disturbance," he said.

"I'd come in. I'd done a little rose pruning—I've retired, you know. And I stood at the end of my front porch there, with an eye on the street—Fay had slipped out somewhere," said Judge McKelva, and bent on her his benign smile that looked so much like a scowl.

"I was only uptown in the beauty parlor, letting Myrtis roll up my hair," said Fay.

"And I saw the fig tree," said Judge McKelva. "The fig tree! Giving off flashes from those old bird-frighteners Becky saw fit to tie on it years back!"

Both men smiled. They were of two generations but

4

the same place. Becky was Laurel's mother. Those little homemade reflectors, rounds of tin, did not halfway keep the birds from the figs in July.

"Nate, you remember as well as I do, that tree stands between my backyard and where your mother used to keep her cowshed. But it flashed at me when I was peering off in the direction of the Courthouse," Judge McKelva went on. "So I was forced into the conclusion I'd started seeing behind me."

Fay laughed—a single, high note, as derisive as a jay's.

"Yes, that's disturbing." Dr. Courtland rolled forward on his stool. "Let's just have a good look."

"*I* looked. I couldn't see anything had got in it," said Fay. "One of those briars might have given you a scratch, hon, but it didn't leave a thorn."

"Of course, my *memory* had slipped. Becky would say it served me right. Before blooming is the wrong time to prune a climber," Judge McKelva went on in the same confidential way; the doctor's face was very near to his. "But Becky's Climber I've found will hardly take a setback."

"Hardly," the doctor murmured. "I believe my sister still grows one now from a cutting of Miss Becky's Climber." His face, however, went very still as he leaned over to put out the lights.

"It's dark!" Fay gave a little cry. "Why did he have to go back there anyway and get mixed up in those brambles? Because I was out of the house a minute?"

"Because George Washington's Birthday is the time-honored day to prune roses back home," said the Doctor's amicable voice. "You should've asked Adele to step over and prune 'em for you."

"Oh, she offered," said Judge McKelva, and dismissed her case with the slightest move of the hand. "I think by this point I ought to be about able to get the hang of it."

Laurel had watched him prune. Holding the shears in both hands, he performed a sort of weighty saraband, with a lop for this side, then a lop for the other side, as though he were bowing to his partner, and left the bush looking like a puzzle.

"You've had further disturbances since, Judge Mac?"

"Oh, a dimness. Nothing to call my attention to it like that first disturbance."

"So why not leave it to Nature?" Fay said. "That's what I keep on telling him."

Laurel had only just now got here from the airport; she had come on a night flight from Chicago. The meeting had been unexpected, arranged over long-distance yesterday evening. Her father, in the old home in Mount Salus, Mississippi, took pleasure in telephoning instead of writing, but this had been a curiously reticent conversation on his side. At the very last, he'd said, "By the way, Laurel, I've been getting a little interference with my *seeing,* lately. I just might give Nate Courtland a chance to see what he can find." He'd added, "Fay says she'll come along and do some shopping."

His admission of self-concern was as new as anything wrong with his health, and Laurel had come flying.

The excruciatingly small, brilliant eye of the instrument hung still between Judge McKelva's set face and the Doctor's hidden one.

Eventually the ceiling lights blazed on again, and Dr. Courtland stood, studying Judge McKelva, who studied him back.

"I *thought* I was bringing you a little something to keep you busy," Judge McKelva said in the cooperating voice in which, before he retired from the bench, he used to hand down a sentence.

"Your right retina's slipped, Judge Mac," Dr. Courtland said.

"All right, you can fix that," said Laurel's father.

"It needs to be repaired without any more waste of precious time."

"All right, when can you operate?"

"Just for a scratch? Why didn't those old roses go on and die?" Fay cried.

"But this eye didn't get a scratch. What happened didn't happen to the outside of his eye, it happened to the inside. The flashes, too. To the part he sees with, Mrs. McKelva." Dr. Courtland, turning from the Judge and Laurel, beckoned Fay to his chart hanging on the wall. Giving out perfume, she walked across to it. "Here's the outside and here's the inside of our eye," he said. He pointed out on the diagram what would have to be done.

Judge McKelva inclined his weight so as to speak to Laurel in her chair below him. "That eye wasn't fooling, was it!" he said.

"I don't see why this had to happen to *me*," said Fay.

Dr. Courtland led the Judge to the door and into the hallway. "Will you make yourself comfortable in my office, sir, and let my nurse bother you with a few more questions?"

When he returned to the examining room he sat in the patient's chair.

"Laurel," he said, "I don't want to do this operation myself." He went on quickly, "I've kept being so sorry about your mother." He turned and gave what might have been his first direct look at Fay. "My family's known his family for such a long time," he told her— a sentence never said except to warn of the unsayable.

"What is the location of the tear?" Laurel asked.

"Close to central," he told her. She kept her eyes on his and he added, "No tumor."

"Before I even let you try, I think I ought to know how good he'll see," said Fay.

"Now, that depends first on where the tear comes," said Dr. Courtland. "And after that on how good a mender the surgeon is, and then on how well Judge Mac will agree to take our orders, and then on the Lord's will. This girl remembers." He nodded toward Laurel.

"An operation's not a thing you just jump into, I know that much," Fay said.

"You don't want him to wait and lose all the vision in that eye. He's got a cataract forming on his other eye," said Dr. Courtland.

Laurel said, "Father has?"

"I found it before I left Mount Salus. It's been coming along for years, taking its time. He's apprised; he thinks it'll hold off." He smiled.

"It's like Mother's. This was the way she started."

"Now, Laurel, I don't have very much imagination," protested Dr. Courtland. "So I go with caution. I was pretty close to 'em, there at home, Judge Mac and Miss Becky both. I stood over what happened to your mother."

"I was there too. You know nobody could blame you, or imagine how you could have prevented anything—"

"If we'd known then what we know now. The eye was just a part of it," he said. "With your mother."

Laurel looked for a moment into the experienced face, so entirely guileless. The Mississippi country that lay behind him was all in it.

He stood up. "Of course, if you ask me to do it, I will," he said. "But I wish you wouldn't ask me."

"Father's not going to let you off," Laurel said quietly.

"Isn't my vote going to get counted at all?" Fay asked, following them out. "I vote we just forget about the whole business. Nature's the great healer."

"All right, Nate," Judge McKelva said, when they had all sat down together in Dr. Courtland's consulting office. "How soon?"

Dr. Courtland said, "Judge Mac, I've just managed to catch Dr. Kunomoto by the coat-tails over in Houston. You know, he taught me. He's got a more radical method now, and he can fly here day after tomorrow—"

"What for?" Judge McKelva said. "Nate, I hied myself away from home and comfort and tracked down here and put myself in your hands for one simple reason: I've got confidence in you. Now show me I'm still not too old to exercise good judgment."

"All right, sir, then that's the way it'll be," Dr. Courtland said, rising. He added, "You know, sir, this operation is not, in any hands, a hundred per cent predictable?"

"Well, I'm an optimist."

"I didn't know there were any more such animals," said Dr. Courtland.

"Never think you've seen the last of anything,"

scoffed Judge McKelva. He answered the Doctor's smile with a laugh that was like the snarl of triumph from an old grouch, and Dr. Courtland, taking the glasses the Judge held on his knees, gently set them back onto his nose.

In his same walk, like a rather stately ploughboy's, the Doctor led them through the jammed waiting room. "I've got you in the hospital, they've reserved me the operating room, and I'm fixed up, too," he said.

"He can move heaven and earth, just ask him to," said his nurse in a cross voice as they passed her in the doorway.

"Go right on over to the hospital and settle in." As the elevator doors opened, Dr. Courtland touched Laurel lightly on the shoulder. "I ordered you the ambulance downstairs, sir—it's a safer ride."

"What's he acting so polite about?" Fay asked, as they went down. "I bet when the bill comes in he won't charge so polite."

"I'm in good hands, Fay," Judge McKelva told her. "I know his whole family."

There was a sharp, cold wind blowing through Canal Street. Back home, Judge McKelva had always set the example for Mount Salus in putting aside his winter hat on Straw Hat Day, and he stood here now in his creamy panama. But though his paunch was bigger, he looked less ruddy, looked thinner in the face than on his wedding day, Laurel thought: this was the last time she had seen him. The mushroom-colored patches under his eyes belonged there, hereditary like the black and overhanging McKelva eyebrows that nearly met in one across his forehead—but what was he seeing? She wondered if through that dilated but benevolent gaze of his he was really quite seeing Fay, or herself, or anybody at all. In the lime-white glare of New Orleans, waiting for the ambulance without questioning the need for it, he seemed for the first time in her memory a man admitting to a little uncertainty in his bearings.

"If Courtland's all that much, he better put in a better claim on how good this is going to turn out," said Fay. "And he's not so perfect—I saw him spank that nurse."

 2

FAY SAT AT THE WINDOW, Laurel stood in the doorway; they were in the hospital room waiting for Judge McKelva to be brought back after surgery.

"What a way to keep his promise," said Fay. "When

he told me he'd bring me to New Orleans some day, it was to see the Carnival." She stared out the window. "And the Carnival's going on right now. It looks like this is as close as we'll get to a parade."

Laurel looked again at her watch.

"He came out fine! He stood it fine!" Dr. Courtland called out. He strode into the room, still in his surgical gown. He grinned at Laurel from a face that poured sweat. "And I think with luck we're going to keep some vision in that eye."

The tablelike bed with Judge McKelva affixed to it was wheeled into the room, and he was carried past the two women. Both his eyes were bandaged. Sandbags were packed about his head, the linen pinned across the big motionless mound of his body close enough to bind him.

"You didn't tell me he'd look like that," said Fay.

"He's fine, he's absolutely splendid," said Dr. Courtland. "He's got him a beautiful eye." He opened his mouth and laughed aloud. He was speaking with excitement, some carry-over of elation, as though he'd just come in from a party.

"Why, you can't hardly tell even who it is under all that old pack. It's big as a house," said Fay, staring down at Judge McKelva.

"He's going to surprise us all. If we can make it stick, he's going to have a little vision he didn't think was coming to him! That's a *beautiful* eye."

"But *look* at him," said Fay. "When's he going to come to?"

"Oh, he's got plenty of time," said Dr. Courtland, on his way.

Judge McKelva's head was unpillowed, lengthening the elderly, exposed throat. Not only the great dark eyes but their heavy brows and their heavy under-shadows were hidden, too, by the opaque gauze. With so much of its dark and bright both taken from it, and with his sleeping mouth as colorless as his cheeks, his face looked quenched.

This was a double room, but Judge McKelva had it, for the time being, to himself. Fay had stretched out a while ago on the second bed. The first nurse had come on duty; she sat crocheting a baby's bootee, so automatically that she appeared to be doing it in her sleep. Laurel moved about, as if to make sure that the room was all in order, but there was nothing to do; not yet. This was like a nowhere. Even what could be seen from the high window might have been the rooftops of any city, colorless and tarpatched, with here and there small mirrors of rainwater. At first, she did not realize she could see the bridge—it stood out there dull in the distance, its function hardly evident, as if it were only another building. The river was not visible. She lowered the blind against the wide white sky that re-flected it. It seemed to her that the grayed-down, anonymous room might be some reflection itself of Judge McKelva's "disturbance," his dislocated vision that had brought him here.

Then Judge McKelva began grinding and gnashing his teeth.

"Father?" Laurel moved near.

"That's only the way he wakes up," said Fay from her bed, without opening her eyes. "I get it every morning."

Laurel stood near him, waiting.

"What's the verdict?" her father presently asked, in a parched voice. "Eh, Polly?" He called Laurel by her childhood name. "What's your mother have to say about me?"

"Look-a-here!" exclaimed Fay. She jumped up and pattered toward his bed in her stockinged feet. "Who's *this?*" She pointed to the gold button over her breastbone.

The nurse, without stopping her crochet hook, spoke from the chair. "Don't go near that eye, hon! Don't nobody touch him or monkey with that eye of his, and don't even touch the bed he's on, till Dr. Courtland says touch, or somebody'll be mighty sorry. And Dr. Courtland will skin me alive."

"That's right," said Dr. Courtland, coming in; then he bent close and spoke exuberantly into the aghast face. "All through with my part, sir! Your part's just starting! And yours will be harder than mine. You got to lie still! No moving. No turning. No tears." He smiled. "No nothing! Just the passage of time. We've got to wait on your eye."

When the doctor straightened, the nurse said, "I wish he'd waited for me to give him a sip of water before he took off again."

"Go ahead. Wet his whistle, he's awake," said Dr. Courtland and moved to the door. "He's just possuming." His finger beckoned Laurel and Fay outside.

"Now listen, you've got to watch him. Starting now. Take turns. It's not as easy as anybody thinks to lie still and nothing else. I'll talk Mrs. Martello into doing private duty at night. Laurel, a good thing you've got the time. He's going to get extra-special care, and we're not running any risks on Judge Mac."

Laurel, when he'd gone, went to the pay telephone in the corridor. She called her studio; she was a professional designer of fabrics in Chicago.

"No point in you staying just because the doctor said so," said Fay when Laurel hung up. She had listened like a child.

"Why, I'm staying for my own sake," said Laurel. She decided to put off the other necessary calls. "Father'll need all the time both of us can give him. He's not very well suited to being tied down."

"O.K., that's not a matter of life and death, is it?" said Fay in a cross voice. As they went back to the room together, Fay leaned over the bed and said, "I'm glad you can't see yourself, hon."

Judge McKelva gave out a shocking and ragged

sound, a snore, and firmed his mouth. He asked, "What's the time, Fay?"

"That sounds more like you," she said, but didn't tell him the time. "It was that old *ether* talking when he came to before," she said to Laurel. "Why, he hadn't even mentioned Becky, till you and Courtland started him."

The Hibiscus was a half hour's ride away on the city's one remaining streetcar line, but through the help of one of the floor nurses, Laurel and Fay were able to find rooms there by the week. It was a decayed mansion on a changing street; what had been built as its twin next door was a lesson to it now: it was far along in the course of being demolished.

Laurel hardly ever saw any of the other roomers, although the front door was never locked and the bathroom was always busy; at the hours when she herself came and went, the Hibiscus seemed to be in the sole charge of a cat on a chain, pacing the cracked-open floral tiles that paved the front gallery. Long in the habit of rising early, she said she would be with her father by seven. She would stay until three, when Fay would come to sit until eleven; Fay could ride the streetcar back in the safe company of the nurse, who lived nearby. And Mrs. Martello said she would take on the private duty late shift for the sake of one living man, that Dr. Courtland. So the pattern was set.

It meant that Laurel and Fay were hardly ever in the same place at the same time, except during the hours when they were both asleep in their rooms at the Hibiscus. These were adjoining—really half rooms; the partition between their beds was only a landlord's strip of wallboard. Where there was no intimacy, Laurel shrank from contact; she shrank from that thin board and from the vague apprehension that some night she might hear Fay cry or laugh like a stranger at something she herself would rather not know.

In the mornings, Judge McKelva ground his teeth, Laurel spoke to him, he waked up, and found out from Laurel how she was and what time her watch showed. She gave him his breakfast; while she fed him she could read him the *Picayune*. Then while he was being washed and shaved she went to her own breakfast in the basement cafeteria. The trick was not to miss the lightning visits of Dr. Courtland. On lucky days, she rode up in the elevator with him.

"It's clearing some," Dr. Courtland said. "It's not to be hurried."

By this time, only the operated eye had to be covered. A hivelike dressing stood on top of it. Judge McKelva seemed inclined to still lower the lid over his good eye. Perhaps, open, it could see the other eye's bandage. He lay as was asked of him, without moving. He never asked about his eye. He never mentioned his eye. Laurel followed his lead.

Neither did he ask about her. His old curiosity

would have prompted a dozen specific questions about how she was managing to stay here, what was happening up in Chicago, who had given her her latest commission, when she would have to go. She had left in the middle of her present job—designing a theatre curtain for a repertory theatre. Her father left his questions unasked. But both knew, and for the same reason, that bad days go better without any questions at all.

He'd loved being read to, once. With good hopes, she brought in a stack of paperbacks and began on the newest of his favorite detective novelist. He listened but without much comment. She went back to one of the old ones they'd both admired, and he listened with greater quiet. Pity stabbed her. Did they *move too fast* for him now?

Part of her father's silence Laurel laid, at first, to the delicacy he had always shown in family feelings. (There had only been the three of them.) Here was his daughter, come to help him and yet wrenched into idleness; she could not help him. Fay was accurate about it: any stranger could tell him the time. Eventually, Laurel saw that her father had accepted her uselessness with her presence all along. What occupied his full mind was time itself; time passing: he was concentrating.

She was always conscious, once she knew, of the effort being made in this room, hour after hour, from his motionless bed; and she was conscious of time along with him, setting her inner chronology with his, more or less as if they needed to keep in step for a long walk ahead of them. The Venetian blind was kept lowered to let in only a two-inch strip of March daylight at the window. Laurel sat so that this light fell into her lap onto her book, and Judge McKelva, holding himself motionless, listened to her read, then turn the page, as if he were silently counting, and knew each page by its number.

The day came when Judge McKelva was asked to share the room with another patient. When Laurel walked in one morning, she saw an old man, older than her father, wearing new, striped cotton pajamas and an old broadbrimmed black felt hat, rocking in the chair by the second bed. Laurel could see the peppering of red road dust on the old man's hat above his round blue eyes.

"This is too strong a light for my father, I'm afraid, sir," she said to him.

"Mr. Dalzell pulled the blind down during the night," said Mrs. Martello, speaking in a nurse's ventriloquist voice. "Didn't you pull it down?" she shrieked. Judge McKelva did not betray that he was awake, but the old man rocking appeared as oblivious as the Judge to the sound of their voices. "He's blind, and nearly deaf in the bargain," Mrs. Martello said proudly. "And he's going in surgery just as soon as they get him all fixed up for it. He's got a malignancy."

"I had to pull the vine down to get the possum," Mr. Dalzell piped up, while Laurel and the nurse struggled together to string the blind back into place. Dr. Courtland came in and did it.

Mr. Dalzell proved to be a fellow Mississippian. He was from Fox Hill. Almost immediately, he convinced himself that Judge McKelva was his long-lost son Archie Lee.

"Archie Lee," he said, "I might've known if you ever did come home, you'd come home drunk."

Judge McKelva once would have smiled. Now he lay as ever, his good eye closed, or open on the ceiling, and had no words to spare.

"Don't you worry about *Mr. Dalzell*," Mrs. Martello said to Laurel as they prepared one morning to change places. "Your daddy just lets Mr. Dalzell rave. He keeps just as still, laying there just like he's supposed to. He's good as gold. *Mr. Dalzell's* nothing you got to worry about."

3

"Nothing to do but give it more time," said Dr. Courtland regularly. "It's clearing. I believe we're getting us
an eye that's going to *see* a little bit."

But although Dr. Courtland paid his daily visits as
to a man recovering, to Laurel her father seemed to be
paying some unbargained-for price for his recovery.
He lay there unchangeably big and heavy, full of effort
yet motionless, while his face looked tireder every
morning, the circle under his visible eye thick as paint.
He opened his mouth and swallowed what she offered
him with the obedience of an old man—obedience! She
felt ashamed to let him act out the part in front of her.
She managed a time or two (by moving heaven and
earth) to have some special dish prepared for him outside; but he might as well have been spooned out hospital grits, canned peaches, and Jello, for all that food
distracted him out of his patience—out of his unnatu-
ral reticence: he had yet to say he would be all right.

One day, she had the luck to detect an old copy of
Nicholas Nickleby on the dusty top shelf in the paper-
back store. That would reach his memory, she believed,
and she began next morning reading it to her father.

He did not ask her to stop; neither could he help her when she lost their place. Of course, she was not able to read aloud with her mother's speed and vivacity—that was probably what he missed. In the course of an hour, he rolled his visible eye her way, though he rationed himself on the one small movement he was permitted, and lay for a long time looking at her. She was not sure he was listening to the words.

"Is that all?" his patient voice asked, when she paused.

"You got that gun loaded yet?" called Mr. Dalzell. "Archie Lee, I declare I want to see you load that gun before they start to coming."

"That's the boy. You go right on hunting all night in your mind," Mrs. Martello stoutly told Mr. Dalzell. She would never in a year dare to get so possessive of Judge McKelva, Laurel reflected, or find something in his predicament that she could joke about. She had gained no clue but one to what he used to be like in Mount Salus. "He's still keeping as good as gold," she greeted Laurel every morning. "It's nothing but goodness—I don't think he *sleeps* all that steady."

Mrs. Martello had crocheted twenty-seven pairs of bootees. Bootees were what she counted. "You'd be surprised how fast I give out of 'em," she said. "It's the most popular present there is."

Judge McKelva had years ago developed a capacity for patience, ready if it were called on. But in this affliction, he seemed to Laurel to lie in a *dream* of patience. He seldom spoke now unless he was spoken to, and then, which was wholly unlike him, after a wait—as if he had to catch up. He didn't try any more to hold her in his good eye.

He lay more and more with both eyes closed. She dropped her voice sometimes, and then sat still.

"I'm not asleep," said her father. "Please don't stop reading."

"What do you think of his prospects now?" Laurel asked Dr. Courtland, following him out into the corridor. "It's three weeks."

"Three weeks! Lord, how they fly," he said. He believed he hid the quick impatience of his mind, and moving and speaking with deliberation he did hide it —then showed it all in his smile. "He's doing all right. Lungs clear, heart strong, blood pressure not a bit worse than it was before. And that eye's clearing. I think he's got some vision coming, just a little bit around the edge, you know, Laurel, but if the cataract catches up with him, I want him seeing enough to find his way around the garden. A little longer. Let's play safe."

Going down on the elevator with him, another time, she asked, "Is it the drugs he has to take that make him seem such a distance away?"

He pinched a frown into his freckled forehead.

"Well, no two people react in just the same way to any-thing." They held the elevator for him to say, "People are different, Laurel."

"Mother was different," she said.

Laurel felt reluctant to leave her father now in the afternoons. She stayed and read. *Nicholas Nickleby* had seemed as endless to her as time must seem to him, and it had now been arranged between them, without words, that she was to sit there beside him and read— but silently, to herself. He too was completely silent while she read. Without being able to see her as she sat by his side, he seemed to know when she turned each page, as though he kept up, through the succession of pages, with time, checking off moment after moment; and she felt it would be heartless to close her book un-til she'd read him to sleep.

One day, Fay came in and caught Laurel sitting up asleep herself, in her spectacles.

"Putting your eyes out, too? I told him if he hadn't spent so many years of his life poring over dusty old books, his eyes would have more strength saved up for now," Fay told her. She sidled closer to the bed. "About ready to get up, hon?" she cried. "Listen, they're hold-ing parades out yonder right now. Look what they threw me off the float!"

Shadows from the long green eardrops she'd come

in wearing made soft little sideburns down her small, intent face as she pointed to them, scolding him. "What's the good of a Carnival if we don't get to go, hon?"

It was still incredible to Laurel that her father, at nearly seventy, should have let anyone new, a beginner, walk in on his life, that he had even agreed to pardon such a thing.

"Father, where did you meet her?" Laurel had asked when, a year and a half ago, she had flown down to Mount Salus to see them married.

"Southern Bar Association." With both arms he had made an expansive gesture that she correctly read as the old Gulf Coast Hotel. Fay had had a part-time job there; she was in the typist pool. A month after the convention, he brought her home to Mount Salus, and they were married in the Courthouse.

Perhaps she was forty, and so younger than Laurel. There was little even of forty in her looks except the line of her neck and the backs of her little square, idle hands. She was bony and blue-veined; as a child she had very possibly gone undernourished. Her hair was still a childish tow. It had the tow texture, as if, well rubbed between the fingers, those curls might have gone to powder. She had round, country-blue eyes and a little feist jaw.

When Laurel flew down from Chicago to be present at the ceremony, Fay's response to her kiss had been to say, "It wasn't any use in you bothering to come so far." She'd smiled as though she meant her scolding to flatter. What Fay told Laurel now, nearly every afternoon at the changeover, was almost the same thing. Her flattery and her disparagement sounded just alike.

It was strange, though, how Fay never called anyone by name. Only she had said "Becky": Laurel's mother, who had been dead ten years by the time Fay could have first heard of her, when she had married Laurel's father.

"What on earth made Becky give you a name like that?" she'd asked Laurel, on that first occasion.

"It's the state flower of West Virginia," Laurel told her, smiling. "Where my mother came from."

Fay hadn't smiled back. She'd given her a wary look.

One later night, at the Hibiscus, Laurel tapped at Fay's door.

"What do you want?" Fay asked as she opened it.

She thought the time had come to know Fay a little better. She sat down on one of the hard chairs in the narrow room and asked her about her family.

"My family?" said Fay. "None of 'em living. That's why I ever left Texas and came to Mississippi. We may not have had much, out in Texas, but we were always so close. Never had any secrets from each other, like some families. Sis was just like my twin. My brothers were all so unselfish! After Papa died, we all gave up everything for Mama, of course. Now that she's gone,

I'm glad we did. Oh, I wouldn't have run off and left anybody that needed me. Just to call myself an artist and make a lot of money."

Laurel did not try again, and Fay never at any time knocked at her door.

Now Fay walked around Judge McKelva's bed and cried, "Look! Look what I got to match my eardrops! How do you like 'em, hon? Don't you want to let's go dancing?" She stood on one foot and held a shoe in the air above his face. It was green, with a stiletto heel. Had the shoe been a written page, some brief she'd concocted on her own, he looked at it in her hands there for long enough to read it through. But he didn't speak.

"But just let me try slipping *out* a minute in 'em, would he ever let me hear about it!" Fay said. She gave him a smile, to show her remark was meant for him to hear. He offered no reply.

Laurel stayed on, until now the supper trays began to rattle.

"Archie Lee, you gonna load that gun or you rather be caught napping?" Mr. Dalzell called out.

"Mr. Dalzell reminds me of my old grandpa," said Fay. "I'm not sorry to have him in here. He's company."

The floor nurse came in to feed Mr. Dalzell, then to stick him with a needle, while Fay helped Judge McKelva with his supper—mostly by taking bite for bite. Laurel stayed on until out in the corridor the lights came on and the room went that much darker.

"Maybe you can sleep now, Father—you haven't been asleep all day," said Laurel.

Fay switched on the night light by the bed. Placed low, and not much more powerful than a candle flame, it touched Judge McKelva's face without calling forth a flicker of change in its patient expression. Laurel saw now that his hair had grown long on the back of his neck, not black but white and featherlike.

"Tell me something you would like to have," Laurel begged him.

Fay, bending down over him, placed her lighted cigarette between his lips. His chest lifted visibly as he drew on it, and after a moment she took it away and his chest slowly fell as the smoke slowly traveled out of his mouth. She bent and gave it to him again.

"*There's* something," she said.

"Don't let the fire go out, son!" called Mr. Dalzell.

"No sir! Everything around this camp's being took good care of, Mr. Dalzell!" yelled the floor nurse, coming to the door. "You just crawl right in your tent and say your prayers good and go to sleep."

Laurel stood, and said goodnight. "Dr. Courtland believes the time's almost here to try your pinhole specs," she dared to add. "Do you hear, Father?"

He, who had been the declared optimist, had not once expressed hope. Now it was she who was offering it to him. And it might be false hope.

There was no response in the room. Judge McKelva,

like Mr. Dalzell, lay in the dark, and Fay crouched in the rocker, one cheek on the windowsill, with a peep on the crack.

Laurel went reluctantly away.

4

It was not that night but the next that Laurel, in her room at the Hibiscus, having already undressed, suddenly dressed again. As she ran down the steps into the warm, uneasy night, the roof light went on in a passing cab. She hailed and ran for it.

"You don't know how lucky you are, sister," said the driver. "Getting you something-to-ride on a night like tonight."

The interior of the cab reeked of bourbon, and as they passed under a streetlight she saw a string of cheap green beads on the floor—a favor tossed from a parade float. The driver took back streets, squeezing around at every corner, it seemed to Laurel, who was straining forward; but when she let down the window glass for air, she heard the same mocking trumpet playing with a band from the same distance away. Then she heard more than one band, heard rival bands playing up distant streets.

Perhaps what she had felt was no more than the atmospheric oppression of a Carnival night, of crowds running wild in the streets of a strange city. And at the very beginning of the day, when she entered her father's room, she thought something had already happened to Mr. Dalzell. He was up on a wheeled table, baldheaded as an infant, hook-nosed and silent—they had taken away his teeth. It was only that something was *going* to happen. A pair of orderlies came during Judge McKelva's breakfast to take Mr. Dalzell to the operating room. As he was wheeled out, no longer vigilant, into the corridor, his voice trailed back, "*Told* you rascals not to let the fire go out." They had still not brought him back when Laurel left.

A strange milky radiance shone in a hospital corridor at night, like moonlight on some deserted street. The whitened floor, the whitened walls and ceiling, were set with narrow bands of black receding into the distance, along which the spaced-out doors, graduated from large to small, were all closed. Laurel had never noticed the design in the tiling before, like some clue she would need to follow to get to the right place. But of course the last door on the right of the corridor, the one standing partway open as usual, was still her father's.

An intense, tight little voice from inside there said at that moment in high pitch, "I tell you enough is enough!"

Laurel was halted. A thousand packthreads seemed to cross and crisscross her skin, binding her there.

The voice said, even higher, "This is my birthday!"

Laurel saw Mrs. Martello go running from the nurse's station into the room. Then Mrs. Martello reappeared, struggling her way backwards. She was pulling Fay, holding her bodily. A scream shot out and ricocheted from walls and ceiling. Fay broke free from the nurse, whirled, and with high-raised knees and white face came running down the corridor. Fists drumming against her temples, she knocked against Laurel as if Laurel wasn't there. Her high heels let off a fusillade of sounds as she passed and hurled herself into the waiting room with voice rising, like a child looking for its mother.

Mrs. Martello came panting up to Laurel, heavy on her rubber heels.

"She laid hands on him! She said if he didn't snap out of it, she'd—" The veneer of nurse slipped from Mrs. Martello—she pushed up at Laurel the red, shocked face of a Mississippi countrywoman as her voice rose to a clear singsong. "She taken ahold of him. She was abusing him." The word went echoing. "I think she was fixing to pull him out of that bed. I think she thought she could! Sure, she wasn't able to move *that* mountain!" Mrs. Martello added wildly,

"*She's* not a nurse!" She swung her starched body around and sent her voice back toward Judge Mc-Kelva's door. "What's the matter with that woman? Does she want to *ruin* your eye?"

At last her legs drove her. Laurel ran.

The door stood wide open, and inside the room's darkness a watery constellation hung, throbbing and near. She was looking straight out at the whole Mississippi River Bridge in lights. She found her way, the night light was burning. Her father's right arm was free of the cover and lay out on the bed. It was bare to the shoulder, its skin soft and gathered, like a woman's sleeve. It showed her that he was no longer concentrating. At the sting in her eyes, she remembered for him that there must be no tears in his, and she reached to put her hand into his open hand and press it gently.

He made what seemed to her a response at last, yet a mysterious response. His whole, pillowless head went dusky, as if he laid it under the surface of dark, pouring water and held it there.

Every light in the room blazed on. Dr. Courtland, a dark shape, shoved past her to the bed. He set his fingertips to her father's wrist. Then his hand passed over the operated eye; with its same delicacy it opened the good eye. He bent over and stared in, without speaking. He knocked back the sheet and laid the side of his head against her father's gowned chest; for a moment his own eyes closed.

It was her father who appeared to Laurel as the one listening. His upper lip had lifted, short and soft as a child's, showing ghostly-pale teeth which no one ever saw when he spoke or laughed. It gave him the smile of a child who is hiding in the dark while the others hunt him, waiting to be found.

Now the doctor's hand swung and drove for the signal button. "Get out in a hurry. And collar his wife and hold her. Both of you go in the waiting room, stay there till I come."

The nurse pushed into the room, with another nurse at her shoulder.

"Now what did *he* pull?" Mrs. Martello cried.

The other nurse whipped the curtains along the rod between the two beds, shutting out Mr. Dalzell's neat, vacated bed and the rocking chair with the felt hat hanging on it. With her toe, she kicked out of her way the fallen window blind lying there on the floor.

Dr. Courtland, using both hands, drew Laurel outside the room. "Laurel, no time to lose." He closed the door on her.

But in the hall, she heard him give an answer to the nurse. "The renegade! I believe he's just plain sneaked out on us."

In the waiting room, Fay stood being patted by an old woman who was wearing bedroom slippers and holding a half-eaten banana in her free hand.

"Night after night, sitting up there with him, putting the food in his mouth, giving him his straw, letting him use up my cigarettes, keeping him from thinking!" Fay was crying on the woman's bosom. "Then to get hauled out by an uppity nurse who doesn't know my business from hers!"

Laurel went up to her. "Fay, it can't be much more serious. The doctor's closed in with Father now."

"Never speak to me again!" shrieked Fay without turning around. "That nurse dragged me and pushed me, and you're the one let her do it!"

"Dr. Courtland wants us to stay here till he calls us."

"You bet I'm staying! Just wait till he hears what I've got to say to him!" cried Fay.

"You pore little woman," said the old woman easily. "Don't they give us all a hard time."

"I believe he's dying," said Laurel.

Fay spun around, darted out her head, and spat at her.

The old woman said, "Now whoa. Why don't you-all take a seat and save your strength? Just wait and let them come tell you about it. They will." There was an empty chair in the circle pulled up around a table, and Fay sat down among five or six grown men and women who all had the old woman's likeness. Their coats were on the table in a heap together, and open shoeboxes and paper sacks stood about on the floor; they were a family in the middle of their supper.

Laurel began walking, past this group and the others

who were sprawled or sleeping in chairs and on couches, past the television screen where a pale-blue group of Westerners silently shot it out with one another, and as far as the door into the hall, where she stood for a minute looking at the clock in the wall above the elevators, then walked her circle again.

The family Fay had sat down with never let the conversation die.

"Go on in there, Archie Lee, it's still your turn," the old woman said.

"I ain't ready to go." A great hulking man in a short coat like a red blanket, who was too gray-headed to be her child, spoke like her child and took a drink from a pint bottle of whiskey.

"They still ain't letting us in but one at a time. It's your turn," the old woman said. She went on to Fay. "You from Mississippi? We're from Mississippi. Most of us claims Fox Hill."

"I'm *not* from Mississippi. I'm from Texas." She let out a long cry.

"Yours been operated on? Ours been operated on," said one of the daughters to Fay. "He's been in intensive care ever since they got through with him. His chances are a hundred to one against."

"Go on in yonder, scare-cat," ordered the mother.

"They went in my husband's eye without consulting my feelings and next they try to run me out of this hospital!" cried Fay.

"Mama, it's Archie Lee's turn, and I come after you. Go yourself," said the daughter.

"I reckon you'll have to excuse me a minute," the old woman said to Fay. She began brushing at her bosom where Fay had cried, shaking herself to get the crumbs off her skirt. "I declare, I'm getting to where I ain't got much left to say to Dad myself."

"You know what his face looks like to me? A piece of paper," said a wizened-looking daughter.

"I ain't going to tell him that," said the old woman.

"Tell him you ain't got too much longer to stay," suggested one of the sons.

"Ask him if he knows who you are," said the wizened-looking daughter.

"Or you can just try keeping your mouth shut," said Archie Lee.

"He's your dad, the same as mine," warned the old woman. "I'm going in because you skipped your turn. Now wait for me! Don't run off and leave me."

"He don't know I'm living," said Archie Lee, as the woman trudged through the doorway in Indian moccasins. He tilted up the bottle: Mr. Dalzell's son, long lost.

Fay sobbed the louder after the old woman went.

"How you like Mississippi?" Mr. Dalzell's family asked, almost in a chorus. "Don't you think it's friendly?" asked the wizened daughter.

"I guess I'm used to Texas."

"Mississippi is the best state in the Union," said Archie Lee and he put his feet up and stretched out full length on the couch.

"I didn't say I didn't have kin here. I had a grandpa living close to Bigbee, Mississippi," Fay said.

"Now you're talking!" the youngest girl said. "We know right where Bigbee is, could find it for you right now. Fox Hill is harder to find than Bigbee. But *we* don't think it's lonesome, because by the time you get all of us together, there's nine of us, not counting the tadpoles. Ten, if Granddad gets over this. He's got cancer."

"Cancer's what my dad had. And Grandpa! Grandpa loved me better than all the rest. That sweet old man, he died in my arms," Fay said, glaring at Laurel across the room. "They died, but not before they did every bit they could to help themselves, and tried all their might to get better, for our sakes. They said they knew, if they just tried hard enough—"

"I always tell mine to have faith," said the wizened daughter.

And as if their vying and trouble-swapping were the order of the day, or the order of the night, in the waiting room, they were all as unaware of the passing of the minutes as the man on the couch, whose dangling hand now let the bottle drop and slide like an empty slipper across the floor into Laurel's path. She walked on, giving them the wide berth of her desolation.

"Wish they'd give Dad something to drink. Wash

his mouth out," said the old mother coming back—
Laurel nearly met her in the door.

"Remember Mamie's boy?" Another family had
come in, grouping themselves around the Coke machine. The man who was working it called out, "He
shot hisself or somebody shot him, one. He begged for
water. The hospital wouldn't give him none. Honey,
he died wanting water."

"I remember Joe Boy Bush from Bruintown," a
man retorted, turning around from the television
screen. "He was laying there going without water and
he reached himself over and bit that tube in two and
drunk that glucose. And drunk ever' drop that was
in it. And that fool, in two weeks he was up out of
that bed and they send him home."

"Two weeks! Guess how long they've held us here!"
cried Fay.

"If they don't give your dad no water by next time
round, tell you what, we'll go in there all together
and pour it down him," promised the old mother. "If
he's going to die, I don't want him to die wanting
water."

"That's talking, Mama."

"Ain't that true, Archie Lee?"

But Archie Lee lay on the couch with his mouth
open.

"There's a fair sight. I'm glad his dad can't walk in
on us and see him," said the old woman. "No, if
Dad's going to die I ain't going to let him die wanting

water!" she insisted, and the others began raggedly laughing.

"We'll pour it down him!" cried the mother. "He ain't going to stand a chance against us!" The family laughed louder, as if there could be no helping it. Some of the other families joined in. It seemed to Laurel that in another moment the whole waiting room would dissolve itself in waiting-room laughter.

Dr. Courtland stood in the doorway, the weight of his watch in his hand.

When Laurel and Fay reached him, he drew them into the elevator hall. The door to Judge McKelva's room stood closed.

"I couldn't save him." He laid a hand on the sleeve of each woman, standing between them. He bent his head, but that did not hide the aggrievement, indignation, that was in his voice. "He's gone, and his eye was healing."

"Are you trying to tell me you let my husband die?" Fay cried.

"He collapsed." Fatigue had pouched the doctor's face, his cheeks hung gray. He kept his touch on their arms.

"You picked my birthday to do it on!" Fay screamed out, just as Mrs. Martello came out of the room. She closed the door behind her. She was carrying a hamper.

She pretended not to see them as she drummed past on her heels.

Laurel felt the Doctor's hand shift to grip her arm; she had been about to go straight to the unattended. He began walking the two women toward the elevators. Laurel became aware that he was in evening clothes.

At the elevator he got in with them, still standing between them. "Maybe we asked too much of him," he said grudgingly. "And yet he didn't have to hold out much longer." He looked protestingly at the lighted floors flashing by. "I'd been waiting to know how well that eye would *see!*"

Fay said, "I knew better than let you go in that eye to start with. That eye was just as bright and cocky as yours is right now. He just took a scratch from an old rose briar! He would have got over that, it would all be forgotten now! Nature would have tended to it. But you thought you knew better!" Without taking her eyes from him, she began crying.

Dr. Courtland looked at her briefly, as if he had seen many like Fay. As they were leaving the elevator among all the other passengers, he looked with the ghost of a smile into Laurel's face. In a moment he said, "He helped me through medical school, kept me going when Daddy died. A sacrifice in those days. The Depression hit and he helped me get my start."

"Some things don't bear going into," Laurel said.

"No," he said. "No." He took off his glasses and put them away, as if he and she had just signed their names to these words. He said then, "Laurel, there's nobody from *home* with you. Would you care to put up with us for the rest of the night? Betty would be so glad. Trouble is, there's goings-on, and of course more to follow. Dell—our oldest girl's eighteen—"

Laurel shook her head.

"I've got my driver waiting outside, though," Dr. Courtland went on. "As soon as you-all finish at the office, I'll send you where you're going, with something for you both to make you sleep."

"All I hope is *you* lay awake tonight and remember how little you were good for!" cried Fay.

He took them on, through the necessary office gates, and when they came outside the hospital into the air and the sounds of city streets and of tonight, he helped them into his car.

"I'll phone Adele," he said to Laurel. That was his sister in Mount Salus. "You can take him home to-morrow." Still he did not turn to go back into the building, but stood there by the car, his hand on the door he had closed. He gave the drawn-out moment up to uselessness. She felt it might have been the hardest thing he had done all day, or all his life.

"I wish I could have saved him," he said.

Laurel touched her hand to the window glass. He waved then, and quickly turned.

"Thank you for nothing!" Fay screamed above the whirr of their riding away.

Laurel was still gearing herself to the time things took. It was slow going through the streets. There were many waits. Now and then the driver had to shout from the wheel before they could proceed.

Fay grabbed Laurel's arm as she would have grabbed any stranger's. "I saw a man—I saw a man and he was dressed up like a skeleton and his date was in a long white dress, with snakes for hair, holding up a bunch of lilies! Coming down the steps of that house like they're just starting out!" Then she cried out again, the longing, or the anger, of her whole life all in her voice at one time, "Is it the Carnival?"

Laurel heard a band playing and another band moving in on top of it. She heard the crowd noise, the unmistakable sound of hundreds, of thousands, of people *blundering*.

"I saw a man in Spanish moss, a whole suit of Spanish moss, all by himself on the sidewalk. He was vomiting right in public," said Fay. "Why did I have to be shown that?"

"Where you come from?" the driver said scornfully. "This here is Mardi Gras *night*."

When they reached there, they found that the Carnival was overflowing the Hibiscus too. Masqueraders were coming and going. The cat was off its chain and let inside; it turned its seamed face to look at them and pranced up the staircase and waited for them on the landing, dressed in a monkey coat sewn with sequins.

"All on my birthday. Nobody told me *this* was what was going to happen to me!" Fay cried before she slammed her door.

Her sobbing, the same two close-together, accusing notes running over and over, went on for a time against the thin sounding-board between the two beds. Laurel lay in the dark waiting for it to reach its end. The house took longer than Fay did to go to sleep; the city longer than the house. Eventually she heard the ludicrous sound of chirping frogs emerge from the now completed excavation next door. Toward morning there was the final, parting shot of a pistol fired far off. Nothing came after that; no echo.

They got away in the afternoon. Judge McKelva's body was on board the smooth New Orleans-Chicago train he had always so enjoyed travelling on; he had taken full pleasure in the starched white damask tablecloths, the real rosebud in the silver vase, the celery crisp on ice, the strawberries fresh from Hammond in their season; and the service. The days of the train itself were numbered now.

In the last car, the two women lay back in chairs in

their compartment partitioned off from the observation section behind. Fay had kicked off her shoes. She lay with her head turned away, not speaking.

Set deep in the swamp, where the black trees were welling with buds like red drops, was one low beech that had kept its last year's leaves, and it appeared to Laurel to travel along with their train, gliding at a magic speed through the cypresses they left behind. It was her own reflection in the windowpane—the beech tree was her head. Now it was gone. As the train left the black swamp and pulled out into the space of Pontchartrain, the window filled with a featureless sky over pale smooth water, where a seagull was hanging with wings fixed, like a stopped clock on a wall. She must have slept, for nothing seemed to have changed before her eyes until the seagull became the hands on the clock in the Courthouse dome lit up in the night above Mount Salus trees.

Fay slept still. When Laurel had to touch her shoulder to wake her, Fay struggled and said, "Oh no, no, not any more!"

Two

✤ I

THE ANCIENT PORTER was already rolling his iron-wheeled wagon to meet the baggage car, before the train halted. All six of Laurel's bridesmaids, as they still called themselves, were waiting on the station platform. Miss Adele Courtland stood out in front of them. She was Dr. Courtland's sister, looking greatly aged. As Laurel went first down the steps, Miss Adele softly placed her hands together, then spread her arms.

"Polly," she said.

"What are you here for?" asked Fay, as Laurel moved from one embrace into another.

"We came to meet you," Tish Bullock said. "And to take you home."

Laurel was aware of the row of lighted windows already sliding away behind her. The train gathered speed as swiftly as it had brought itself to a halt. It went out of sight while the wagon, loaded with the long box now, and attended by a stranger in a business suit, was wheeled slowly back along the platform and steered to where a hearse, backed in among the cars, stood with its door wide.

"Daddy wanted to come, Laurel, but we've been trying to spare him," said Tish, with protective eyes following what was happening to the coffin. Her arm was linked in Laurel's.

"I'm Mr. Pitts, hope you remember me," said the businessman, appearing at Laurel's other side. "Now what would you like done with your father?" When she didn't speak, he went on, "May we have him in our parlor? Or would you prefer him to repose at the residence?"

"My father? Why—at his home," said Laurel, stammering.

"At the residence. Until the hour of services. As was the case with the first Mrs. McKelva," said the man.

"I'm Mrs. McKelva now. If you're the undertaker, you do your business with me," said Fay.

Tish Bullock winked at Laurel. It was a moment before she remembered: this was the bridesmaids' automatic signal in moments of acute joy or distress, to show solidarity.

There was a deep boom, like the rolling in of an ocean wave. The hearse door had been slammed shut.

"—and you may have him back in the morning by ten A.M.," the undertaker was saying to Fay. "But first, me and you need to have a little meeting of the minds in a quiet, dignified place where you can be given the opportunity—"

"You bet your boots," said Fay.

The hearse pulled away, then. It turned to the left on Main Street, blotted out the Courthouse fence, and disappeared behind the Presbyterian Church.

Mr. Pitts turned to make his bow to Laurel. "I'll return this lady to you by-and-by," he said.

Miss Adele took Laurel's coat over her arm and the bridesmaids gathered up all the suitcases. The old Bullock Chrysler had been waiting.

It was first-dark in the town of Mount Salus. They turned right on Main Street and drove the three and a half blocks.

The McKelva house was streaming light from every window, upstairs and down. As Tish passed the row of parked cars and turned up into the driveway, Laurel saw that the daffodils were in bloom, long streamers of them reaching down the yard, hundreds of small white trumpets. Tish lightly touched the horn, and the front door opened and still more light streamed out, in which the solid form of Miss Tennyson Bullock walked out and stood on the porch.

Laurel ran from the car and across the grass and up the front steps. Miss Tennyson—Tish's mother—was calling to her in ringing tones, "And he was such a precious, after all!" She folded Laurel close.

Half a dozen—a dozen—old family friends had been waiting here in the house. They came out into the hall from the rooms on both sides as Laurel walked in. Most of them had practiced-for smiles on their faces, and they all called her "Laurel McKelva," just as they always called her. Here at his own home, inside his own front door, there was nobody who seemed to be taken by surprise at what had happened to Judge McKelva. Laurel seemed to remember that Presbyterians were good at this.

But there was a man's deep groan from the dining room, and Major Bullock came swinging out into the hall, cutting through the welcomers, protesting. "I'm not even going to *have* it, I say. He was never sick a day in his life!" Laurel went to meet him and kissed his flushed cheek.

He was the only man here. It might have been out of some sense of delicacy that the bridesmaids and the older ladies, those who were not already widows, had all made their husbands stay home tonight. Miss Tennyson, who had relieved Laurel of her handbag and crushed gloves, smoothed back the part into her hair. She had been Laurel's mother's oldest friend, the first person she'd met when she came to Mount Salus as a bride.

Now she gave a sidelong glance at Tish and asked her, "Did Mr. Pitts manage to catch Fay?"

"He's going to return her to us by-and-by." Tish mocked him perfectly.

"Poor little woman! How is she taking it, Laurel?" asked Major Bullock.

At last she said, "I don't think I can safely predict about Fay."

"Let's not make Laurel try," suggested Miss Adele Courtland.

Miss Tennyson led Laurel into the dining room. The bridesmaids had been setting out a buffet. On the little side table, where Major Bullock, standing with his back to them, was quickly finishing up something, was the drinks tray with some bottles and glasses. Laurel found herself sitting at her old place at the dinner table, the only one seated, while everybody else was trying to wait on her. Miss Tennyson stood right at her shoulder, to make her eat.

"What are all these people doing in my house?"

That was Fay's voice in the hall.

"You've got pies three deep in the pantry, and an icebox ready to pop," said Miss Tennyson, going out to meet her. "And a dining room table that might keep you from going to bed hungry."

"Well, I didn't know I was giving a reception," said Fay. She came as far as the dining room doors and stared in.

"We're Laurel's friends, Fay," Tish reminded her. "The six of us right here, we were her bridesmaids."

"A lot of good her bridesmaids will ever do me. And who's making themselves at home in my parlor?" She crossed the hall.

"Fay, those are the last, devoted remnants of the old Garden Club, of which I'm now president," said Miss Tennyson. "Here now for—for Laurel's mother's sake."

"What's Becky's Garden Club got to do with me?" exclaimed Fay. She stuck her head inside the parlor door and said, "The funeral's not till tomorrow."

"They're a hard bunch to put off till tomorrow," said Miss Tennyson. "They picked their flowers and they brought 'em."

Laurel left her chair and went out to Miss Tennyson

and the gathering ladies. "They're all Father's friends, Fay. They're exactly the ones he'd have counted on to be here in the house to meet us," she said. "And I count on them."

"Well, it's evermore unfair. I haven't got anybody to count on but me, myself, and I." Fay's eyes travelled to the one man in the gathering and she accused him. "*I* haven't got one soul." She let out a cry, and streaked up the stairs.

"Poor little woman, she's the helpless kind," said Major Bullock. "We're going to have to see about her." He looked around him, and there were the suitcases, still standing near the front door. Three of them: one was Judge McKelva's. Major Bullock loaded himself and walked upstairs with them. When he came back, almost immediately, his step was even heavier. Straight-armed, he carried at full length on its hanger a suit of black winter clothes. It swayed more widely than he swayed in negotiating the turn on the landing. There was a shoebox in his other hand and a leather case under his arm.

"She's sending me down to Pitts', Tennyson," he said. "Carrying him these."

"Naked through the streets?" Miss Tennyson objected. "But I suppose you couldn't let her go to the trouble of packing them."

"A man wanted to get on out of the room," he said stiffly. But his arm gave at the elbow, and the suit for a moment sagged; the trousers folded to the floor. He stood there in the middle of the women and cried. He said, "I just can't believe it yet! Can't believe Clint's gone for good and Pitts has got him down there—"

"All right, I'll believe it for you," said Miss Tennyson, on her way to him. She rescued the suit and hung it over his arm for him, so that it was less clumsy for him and looked less like a man. "Now go on and do like she told you. You *insisted* on being here tonight!"

Upstairs, the bedroom door was rather weakly slammed. Laurel had never heard it slammed before. She went and laid her cheek for a moment against Major Bullock's, aware of the tears on it and the bourbon on his breath. He propelled himself forward and out of the lighted house.

"Daddy, wait! I'll drive you!" Tish called, running.

It was the break-up, and when they'd all said goodnight, promising to return in the morning in plenty of time, Laurel saw them to the door and stood waiting until their cars had driven away. Then she walked back through the parlor as far as the doorway into the library behind it. There was her father's old chair sitting up to his desk.

The sound of plates being laid carefully one on top of the other reached her then from the kitchen. She walked in through the pantry.

"It's I."

Laurel knew that would be Miss Adele Courtland. She had finished putting the food away and washing the dishes; she was polishing dry the turkey platter. It was a piece of the old Haviland in the small arbutus pattern—the "laurel"—that Laurel's mother had loved.

"Here in the kitchen it will all start over so soon," Miss Adele said, as if asking forgiveness.

"You can't help being good. That's what Father said about you in New Orleans," Laurel said. Then, "*He* was the best thing in the world too—Dr. Courtland."

Miss Adele nodded her head.

"What happened was not to Father's eye at all. Father was going to see," Laurel told her. "Dr. Courtland was right about the eye. He did everything right." Miss Adele nodded, and Laurel finished, "What happened wasn't like what happened to Mother."

Miss Adele lifted the stacked clean dishes off the kitchen table and carried them into the dining room and put them away in their right places on the shelves of the china closet. She arranged the turkey platter to stand in its groove at the back of the gravy bowl. She put the glasses in, and restored the little wine glasses to their ring around the decanter, with its mended glass stopper still intact. She shut the shivering glass door gently, so as not to rock the old top-heavy cabinet.

"People live their own way, and to a certain extent I almost believe they may die their own way, Laurel." She turned around, and the chandelier threw its light down on her. Her fine-drawn, elegant face might almost have withered a little more while she was out here with the kitchen to herself. She wore her faded hair as she had always worn it from the day when she was Laurel's first-grade teacher, in a Psyche knot. Her voice was as capable of authority as ever. "Sleep, now, Laurel. We'll all be back here in the morning, and you know we won't be the only ones. Goodnight!"

She left by the kitchen door, as always, and stepped home through the joining backyards. It was dark and fragrant out there. When the Courtland kitchen light went on, Laurel closed her back door too, and walked through the house putting out lights. The only illumination on the stairs came from the lamp that they had turned on for her by her bed.

In her own room, she undressed, raised the window, got into bed with the first book her fingers found, and lay without opening it.

The quiet of the Mount Salus night was a little different now. She could hear traffic on some new highway, a sound like the buzzing of one angry fly against a windowpane, over and over.

When Laurel was a child, in this room and in this bed where she lay now, she closed her eyes like this and the rhythmic, nighttime sound of the two beloved reading voices came rising in turn up the stairs every night to reach her. She could hardly fall asleep, she tried to keep awake, for pleasure. She cared for her own books, but she cared more for theirs, which meant their voices. In the lateness of the night, their two voices reading to each other where she could hear them, never letting a silence divide or interrupt them, combined into one unceasing voice and wrapped her around as she listened, as still as if she were asleep. She was sent to sleep under a velvety cloak of words, richly patterned and stitched with gold, straight out of a fairy tale, while they went reading on into her dreams.

Fay slept farther away tonight than in the Hibiscus—they could not hear each other in this house—but nearer in a different way. She was sleeping in the bed where Laurel was born; and where her mother had died. What Laurel listened for tonight was the striking of the mantel clock downstairs in the parlor. It never came.

 2

AT THE INEVITABLE HOUR, Laurel started from her bed and went downstairs in her dressing gown. It was a clear, bright seven o'clock, with morning shadows dappling the shine of the floors and the dining room table. And there was Missouri, standing in her hat and coat in the middle of the kitchen.

"Am I supposed to believe what I hear?" asked Missouri.

Laurel went to her and took her in her arms.

Missouri took off her hat and coat and hung them on the nail with her shoulder bag. She washed her hands, and then she shook out a fresh apron, just as she'd started every morning off during Laurel's mother's life in Mount Salus.

"Well, *I'm* here and *you're* here," said Missouri. It was the bargain to give and take comfort. After a moment's hesitation, Missouri went on, "*He* always want Miss Fay to have her breakfast in bed."

"Then you'll know how to wake her," said Laurel. "When you take it up. Do you mind?"

"Do it for him," said Missouri. Her face softened. "He mightily enjoyed having him somebody to spoil."

In a little while, just as Missouri walked out with the tray, Miss Adele Courtland came in at the back door. She was wearing her best—of course, she'd arranged not to teach her children today. She offered Laurel a double-handful of daffodils, the nodding, gray-white kind with the square cup.

"You know who gave me mine—hers are blooming outside. Silver Bells," Miss Adele prompted her. "Is there a place left to put them?"

They walked through the dining room and across to the parlor. The whole house was filled with flowers; Laurel was seeing them for the first time this morning—the cut branches of Mount Salus prunus

and crab, the thready yellow jasmine, bundles of nar-
cissus, in vases and pitchers that came, along with the
flowers, from houses up and down the street.

"Father's desk—?"

"Miss Laurel, I keep a-calling Miss Fay but she don't
sit up to her breakfast!" called Missouri on the stairs.

"Your day has started, Laurel," said Miss Adele. "I'm
here to answer the door."

Laurel went up, knocked, and opened the door into
the big bedroom. Instead of her mother's writing cabinet that used to stand between those windows, the bed
faced her. It seemed to swim in a bath of pink light.
The mahogany headboard, rising high as the mantel-
piece, had been quilted from top to bottom in peach
satin; peach satin ruffles were thrown back over the
foot of the bed; peach satin smothered the windows
all around. Fay slept in the middle of the bed, deep
under the cover, both hands curled into slack fists above
her head. Laurel could not see her face but only the
back of her neck, the most vulnerable part of anybody,
and she thought: Is there any sleeping person you can
be entirely sure you have not misjudged? Then she
saw the new green shoes placed like ornaments on top
of the mantel shelf.

"Fay!" she cried.

Fay gave no sign.

"Fay, it's morning."

"You go back to sleep."

"This is Laurel. It's a few minutes before ten o'clock. There'll be callers downstairs, asking for you."

Fay pushed herself up on her arms and cried over her shoulder, "I'm the widow! They can all wait till I get there."

"A good breakfast do you a lot of good," said Missouri, bringing it in, letting Laurel out.

Laurel bathed, dressed. A low thunder travelled through the hall downstairs and shook in her hand as she tried to put the pins in her hair. One voice dominated the rest: Miss Tennyson Bullock was taking charge.

"So this time it's Clint's turn to bring you home," said an old lady's voice to her as she came down the stairs. All Laurel could remember of her, the first moment, was that a child's ball thrown over her fence was never to be recovered.

"Yes, daughters need to stay put, where they can keep a better eye on us old folks," said Miss Tennyson Bullock, meeting Laurel at the foot of the stairs with a robust hug. "Honey, he's come."

Miss Tennyson led the way into the parlor. Everything was dim. All over the downstairs, the high old windows had had their draperies drawn. In the parlor, lamps were burning by day and Laurel felt as she entered the room that the furniture was out of place. A number of people rose to their feet and stood still, making a path for her.

The folding doors between the parlor and the library behind it had been rolled all the way back, and the casket was installed across this space. It had been raised on a sort of platform that stood draped with a curtain, a worn old velvet curtain, only halfway hiding the wheels. A screen of florist's ferns was being built up before her eyes behind the coffin. Then a man stepped out from behind the green and presented a full, square face with its small features pulled to the center—what Laurel's mother had called "a Baptist face."

"Miss Laurel, I'm Mr. Pitts again. I recall your dear mother so clearly," he said. "And I believe you're going to be just as pleased now, with your father." He put out his hand and raised the lid.

Judge McKelva lay inside in his winter suit. All around him was draped the bright satin of a jeweler's box, and its color was the same warm, foolish pink that had smothered the windows and spilled over the bed upstairs. His large face reflected the pink, so that his long, heavy cheek had the cast of a seashell, or a pearl. The dark patches underneath his eyes had been erased like traces of human error. Only the black flare of the nostrils and the creases around the mouth had been left him of his old saturnine look. The lid had been raised only by half-section, to show him propped on the pillow; below the waist he lay cut off from any eyes. He was still not to be mistaken for any other man.

"You must close it," said Laurel quietly to Mr. Pitts.

"You're not pleased?" But he had never displeased anyone, his face said.

"Oh, look," said Miss Tennyson, arriving at Laurel's side. "Oh, *look*."

"I don't want it open, please," said Laurel to Mr. Pitts. She touched Miss Tennyson's hand. "But Father would never allow—when Mother died, he protected her from—"

"Your mother was different," said Miss Tennyson firmly.

"He was respecting her wishes," Laurel said. "Not to make her lie here in front of people's eyes—"

"And I've never forgiven him for that. Nobody ever really got to tell Becky goodbye," Miss Tennyson was saying at the same time. "But honey, your father's a Mount Salus man. He's a McKelva. A public figure. You can't deprive the public, can you? Oh, he's lovely."

"I would like him away from their eyes," said Laurel.

"It is Mrs. McKelva's desire that the coffin be open," said Mr. Pitts.

"See there? You can't deprive Fay," said Miss Tennyson. "That settles that." She held out her arms, inviting the room.

Laurel took up her place in front of the coffin, near the head, and stood to meet them as they came.

First they embraced her, and then they stood and looked down at her father. The bridesmaids and their husbands, the whole crowd of them, had gone from the first grade through high school graduation together, and they still stood solid. So did her father's crowd—the County Bar, the elders of the church, the Hunting and Fishing Club cronies; though they seemed to adhere to their own kind, they slowly moved in place, as if they made up the rim of a wheel that slowly turned itself around the hub of the coffin and would bring them around again.

"May I see him?" the Presbyterian minister's wife asked right and left as she elbowed her way in, as if Judge McKelva's body were the new baby. She gazed on him lying there, for a minute. "And here I'd been waiting to see who it was I was saving my Virginia ham for," she said, turning to Laurel and squeezing her around the waist. "It was *your mother* first told me how I could harness one of those and get it cooked so it was fit for anybody to eat. Well, it's headed right for your kitchen." She nodded back to the coffin. "I'm afraid my husband's running a little late. You know people like *this* don't die every day in the week. He's sitting home in his bathrobe now, tearing his hair, trying to do him justice."

"Why, here's Dot," said Miss Adele, posted at the front door.

To everyone in town, she was known simply as Dot. She came in with her nonchalant, twenties stalk on her high heels.

"I couldn't resist," she said in her throaty baritone as she approached the coffin.

She must have been seventy. She had been Judge Mc-

Kelva's private secretary for years and years. When he retired, her feelings had been hurt. Of course, he'd seen to it that she was eased into another job, but she had never forgiven him.

"When I first came to work for him," said Dot, looking at him now, "I paid thirty-five dollars of my salary to a store in Jackson for a set of Mah Johng. It was on sale from a hundred dollars. I really can't to this very day understand myself. But, 'Why, Dot,' this sweet man says, 'I don't see anything so specially the matter with giving yourself a present. I hope you go ahead and enjoy it. Don't reproach yourself like that. You're distressing my ears,' he says. I'll never forget his kind words of advice."

"*Mah Johng!*" gasped Miss Tennyson Bullock. "Great Day in the Morning, I'd forgotten about it."

Dot gave her a bitter look, almost as if she'd said she'd forgotten about Judge McKelva. "Tennyson," she said across his body, "I'm never going to speak to you again."

Somebody had lit the fire, although the day was mild and the room close now, filling with more and more speaking, breathing people.

"Yes, a fire seemed called for," said Major Bullock. He came up to Laurel and scraped his face against hers as though his were numb. His breath had its smell of Christmas morning—it was whiskey. "Fairest, most impartial, sweetest man in the whole Mississippi Bar," he said, his gaze wavering, seeming to avoid Judge Mc-

Kelva's face, going only to the hand that had been placed like a closed satchel at his tailored side. "How soon is that poor little woman going to bring herself downstairs?"

"Eventually," Miss Tennyson told him. Whatever she said, in times of trouble, took on all the finality in the world. Finality was what made the throb in her voice.

 3

"Now WHAT COULD *they* want," said old Mrs. Pease, who stood at the front window parting the draperies.

"Polly," warned Miss Adele.

Everyone turned, and those seated stood up, as two equally fat women and a man walked past Miss Adele into the parlor.

"I said this had to be the right spot, because it looks like the very house to hold a big funeral," said the old fat woman. "Where's Wanda Fay? I don't see her."

While she was speaking, the two women, old and young, were walking up to the coffin, and while they passed it, they looked in. Laurel heard herself being introduced by one of the strangers to the other.

"Mama, this is Judge and Becky's daughter," said the young woman.

"Becky's the one she takes after, then," said the mother, seating herself in Judge McKelva's smoking chair, which now stood nearest the casket. "You don't favor him," she told Laurel. "A grand coffin my little girl's afforded. Makes me jealous." She turned toward the man. "Bubba, this is Judge and Becky's daughter."

The man with them raised his arm from the elbow and waved at Laurel from close range. He wore a windbreaker. "Hi."

"I'm Mrs. Chisom from Madrid, Texas. I'm Wanda Fay's mother," the fat lady said to Laurel. "And this is some of my other children—Sis, from Madrid, Texas, and Bubba, from Madrid, Texas. We got a few others that rather not come in."

"Well, you're news to me," said Miss Tennyson, as if that were simply all there was to it.

Major Bullock came forward to greet them. "I'm Major Bullock!"

"Well, if you're wondering how long it took us, I made it from Madrid in close on to eight hours," the man in the windbreaker said. Madrid was pronounced with the accent as in Mildred. "Crossed the river at Vicksburg. And we're going to have to turn around and go right back. The kids wanted to all pile in, but their mama said you don't ever know what germs they might pick up in a strange place. And she's right. So I left 'em with her in the trailer, and didn't bring but one of 'em. Where's Wendell?"

"I reckon he's looking over the house," said the young woman. She was pregnant, rather than fat.

"Sis brought the whole brood of hers. Sis," said the man. "This is his first wife's daughter."

"I knew that's who she was, you didn't have to introduce us. Feel like I know you already," said the sister to Laurel.

And oddly, Laurel felt that too. Fay had said they didn't even exist, and yet it seemed to Laurel that she had seen them all before.

"I told my bunch they could just play outside in the front yard and watch for us all to come out," said Sis. "That seemed to pretty well satisfy 'em."

Old Mrs. Pease was already at the window curtains, and patting her foot as she peeped out between them.

Major Bullock looked gratified. "I summoned 'em up without any trouble at all," he said. "They were delighted to come." He threw a hopeful glance into the hall.

"You just forgot to warn *us,*" said Miss Tennyson.

Laurel felt a finger twine its way around her own finger, scratch under the ring. "You have bad luck with *your* husband, too?" Mrs. Chisom asked her.

"Year after she married him," said old Mrs. Pease. "Gone. The war. U.S. Navy. Body never recovered."

"*You* was *cheated*," Mrs. Chisom pronounced.

Laurel tried to draw back her finger. Mrs. Chisom let it go in order to poke her in the side as if to shame her. "So you ain't got father, mother, brother, sister, husband, chick nor child. Not a soul to call on, that's you."

"What do you mean! This girl here's surrounded by her oldest friends!" The Mayor of Mount Salus stood there, clapping Laurel on the shoulder. "And listen further: bank's closed, most of the Square's agreed to close for the hour of services, county offices closed. Courthouse has lowered its flag out front, school's letting out early. That ought to satisfy anybody that comes asking who she's got!"

"Friends are here today and gone tomorrow," Mrs. Chisom told Laurel and the Mayor. "Not like your kin. Hope the Lord don't ask me to outlive mine. I'd be much obliged if He'd take *me* the next round. Ain't that a good idea, children?"

A little boy came into the room at a trot while she waited for an answer. He did not look at her or anybody else. He was wearing a cowboy suit and hat and double pistol holsters. He stopped when he saw where he was going.

"Wendell, you pull off your hat if you go any closer," said Sis.

The child bared his head, continued to the coffin, and stood there on tiptoe, at Laurel's side. His mouth opened. He was about seven, fair and frail. The ferocious face he looked at and his own, so near together, were equally unguarded.

"How come he wanted to dress up?" asked the child.

"Who promised if they could come in the house they wouldn't ask questions?" asked Sis.

"Yes, me and my brood believes in clustering just as close as we can get," said Mrs. Chisom. "Bubba pulled his trailer right up in my yard when he married and Irma can string her clothesline as far out as she pleases. Sis here got married and didn't even try to move away. Duffy just snuggled in."

"What's his name?" asked Wendell.

"Wendell, run up those stairs and see if you can find your Aunt Wanda Fay. Tell her to come on down and see who she's got waiting on her," said Bubba.

"I don't want to," said Wendell.

"What you scared of? Nothing's going to bite you upstairs. Go hunt her," said his father.

"I don't want to."

"She better hurry if she wants to see us," Bubba said. "Because we're gonna have to turn right around in a minute and start back to Madrid."

"Now, wait!" said Major Bullock. "You're one of the pallbearers."

"What did he call you, Dad?" cried Wendell.

"It seemed only right," Major Bullock said to the room.

"Tell her to come double-quick," said Bubba to Wendell. "Run!"

"I want to stay here," said Wendell.

"I'm sorry. This is his first funeral," said Sis to Laurel.

"Let me show you Judge," Mrs. Chisom said placatingly to Bubba.

"I just finished seeing him," Bubba said. "I couldn't help but think he's young-looking for a man pushing seventy-one."

"That's right. Not a bit wasted. I'm proud for you, Wanda Fay," Mrs. Chisom said, addressing the ceiling over her head. "Your pa was wasted and they didn't have the power to hide it." She turned to Laurel. "But I reckon he'd lasted longer on nothing but tap water than anybody ever lasted before. Tap water, that's all Mr. Chisom could get down. I kept listening for some complaint out of him, never got one. He had cancer but he didn't whimper about it, not to me. That's because we both of us come from good old Mississippi stock!"

A big, apple-cheeked woman in a hairy tam smiled into Laurel's face from the other side. "I remember, oh, I remember how many Christmases I was among those present in this dear old home in all its hospitality."

This caller was out of her mind, yet even she was not being kept back from Judge McKelva's open coffin. By the rundown heels on her shoes as she lumbered toward her, Laurel knew her for the sewing woman. She would come to people's houses and spend the whole day upstairs at the sewing machine, listening and talking and repeating and getting everything crooked. Miss Verna Longmeier.

"And they'd throw open those doors between these double parlors and the music would strike up! And then—"Miss Verna drew out her arm as though to measure a yard—"then Clinton and I, we'd lead out the dance," she said.

In Mount Salus nobody ever tried to contradict Miss Verna Longmeier. If even a crooked piece of stitching were pointed out to her, she was apt to return: "Let him who is without sin cast the first stone."

"Oh, I've modeled myself on this noble Roman," declared the Mayor, sending out his palm above the casket. "And when I reach higher office—" He strode off to join the other members of the Bar. Laurel saw that they were all sitting more or less together on a row of dining room chairs, like some form of jury.

Miss Thelma Frierson creaked over the floor and stood above the casket. She had filled out the fishing and hunting licenses at her Courthouse window for years and years. Her shoulders drooped as she said, "He had a wonderful sense of humor. Underneath it all."

"Underneath it all, Father knew it *wasn't* funny," said Laurel politely.

"Too bad he ever elected to go to the hospital," old Mrs. Chisom said. "If he knew what ain't funny."

"I tell you, what they let go on in hospitals don't

hardly bear repeating," said Sis. "Irma says the maternity ward in Amarillo would curl your hair."

"Doctors don't know what they're doing. They just know how to charge," said Bubba.

"And you know who I wouldn't trust for a blessed second behind my back? Nurses!" cried Mrs. Chisom.

Laurel looked over their heads, to where the Chinese prints brought home by an earlier generation of missionary McKelvas hung in their changeless grouping around the mantel clock. And she saw that the clock had stopped; it had not been wound, she supposed, since the last time her father had done duty by it, and its hands pointed to some remote three o'clock, as motionless as the time in the Chinese prints. She wanted to go to the clock and take the key from where her father kept it—on a small nail he'd hammered, a little crookedly, into the papered wall—and wind the clock and set it going at the right time. But she could not spare the moment from his side. She felt as though in death her father had been asked to bear the weight of that raised lid himself, and hold it up by lying there, the same way he'd lain on the hospital bed and counted the minutes and the hours to make his life go by. She stood by the coffin as she had sat by his bed, waiting it out with him. Unable to hear the ticking of the clock, she listened to the gritting and the hissing of the fire.

Dr. Woodson was saying, "Clint and me used to take off as shirt-tail lads with both our dogs and be gone all day up in the woods—you know where they used to call it Top o' the World? With the gravel pit dug out of the claybanks there. I've been his doctor for years, hell, we're the same age, but after all this time it hasn't been until now that something made me think about his foot. Clint went swinging on a vine, swinging too wide and too high, and soared off and came down on a piece of tin barefooted. He liked-to bled to death a mile from home! I reckon I must have carried Clint into town on my back and used strength I didn't know I had. You know Clint always gave you the impression you couldn't kill him, that nothing could, but I believe he really must have been kind of delicate."

Light laughter broke out in the room and hushed itself in the same instant.

"Is this it, Aunt Sis?" Wendell Chisom asked. "Is it the funeral yet?"

"It'll be the funeral when I say so," said Sis.

"After I'd *got* him here, he fell out cold. But there's houses in sight by then. It's where the Self-Serve Car Wash is now. I reckon I'm to blame for saving Clint's life for him that time!"

"Father *was* delicate," said Laurel.

"With everything that's the matter with me, you'd have thought he'd outlive me," the doctor went on.

"Not for me or you to ask the reason why," Mrs. Chisom told him. "It's like the choice between Grandpa and my oldest boy Roscoe. Nobody in Texas could understand what the Lord meant, taking Roscoe when He did."

"What happened to Roscoe, Grandma?" Wendell asked, abandoning the coffin to hang over her lap and look up into her face.

"Son, you've heard me tell it. Stuffed up the windows, stuffed up the door, turned on all four eyes of the stove and the oven," said Mrs. Chisom indulgently. "Fire Department drug him out, rushed him to the Baptist Hospital in the firewagon, tried all their tricks, but they couldn't get ahead of Roscoe. He was in Heaven already."

"He beat the fire engines? Was you there, Grandma?" Wendell cried. "You see him beat 'em?"

"I'm his mother. Well, his mother could sit and be thankful he didn't do nothing any more serious to harm his looks. He hated more than anything having remarks made against him. In his coffin he was pretty as a girl. Honey, he just stretched him out easy and put his head on a pillow and waited till he'd quit breathing. Don't you ever let me hear you tried that, Wendell," said Mrs. Chisom.

Wendell turned and looked back at Judge McKelva.

"Roscoe told his friends in Orange, Texas, what he was figuring on doing. When it's all done, they wrote and told me he'd called 'em up crying and they went and cried with him. 'Cried *with* him?' I wrote those people back. 'Why couldn't you-all have told his mother?' I can't get *over* people. I says on my card, 'I had the bus fare. I'm not that poor. I had the round-trip from Madrid to Orange and back again.' " She was patting both feet.

"He's better off, Mama," said Sis. "Better off, just like Judge McKelva laying yonder. Tell yourself the same thing I do."

"I wrote another card and said at least tell his mother what had been fretting my son, if they knew so much, and they finally got around to answering that Roscoe didn't *want* me to know," Mrs. Chisom said, her face arranging itself all at once into an expression of innocence. It lasted for only a minute. She went on, "Roscoe was my mainstay when Mr. Chisom went. They said, 'Prepare your mind, Mrs. Chisom. Mr. Chisom is not going to go anywhere but downhill.' They was guessing right, that time, the doctors was. He went down fast and we buried him back in Mississippi, back in Bigbee, and there on the spot I called Roscoe to me." She pulled Wendell to her now. " 'Roscoe,' I says, 'you're the mainstay now,' I says. 'You're the head of the Chisom family.' He was so happy."

Wendell began to cry. Laurel wanted at that moment to reach out for him, put her arms around him —to guard him. He was like a young, undriven, unfalsifying, unvindictive Fay. So Fay might have appeared, just at the beginning, to her aging father, with his slipping eyesight.

At that moment, Wendell broke from Mrs. Chisom

and ran tearing toward the hallway. He threw his arms around the knees of an old man whom Miss Adele was just showing in from the hall.

"Grandpa Chisom! I can't believe my eyes! It's Grandpa!" Sis cried out.

Wendell at his side, the old man came slowly into the parlor and through the crowd, carrying a yellowed candy box in one hand and a paper sack in the other. Wendell had possession of his old black hat. He came up to Laurel and said, "Young lady, I carried you some Bigbee pecans. I thought you might not harvest their like around here. They're last year's." He held onto his parcels while he explained that he had sat up most of last night, after walking to the crossroads to flag down the bus at three this morning, and had shelled the nuts on the way, to keep awake. "Where I got lost was after I got inside of Mount Salus," he said, giving the box to Laurel. "That's the meats. You can just throw the shells away for me," he added, handing her the sack. "I didn't like to leave 'em in that nice warm seat for the next passenger." He carefully dusted his hands before he turned toward the casket.

"Who you think it is, Grandpa?" asked Wendell.

"It's Mr. McKelva. I reckon he stood whatever it was long enough," said Mr. Chisom. "I'm sorry he had to go while he's so many miles short of home."

"Out of curiosity, who does he remind you of?" Mrs. Chisom asked him as he gazed down.

The old man reflected for a minute. "Nobody," he said.

"Clint thought it was too good a joke not to play it on somebody!" Laurel heard behind her, at the end of a long spate of words.

She saw that most of the Bar had gathered themselves up and gone behind the screen of ferns, without being missed. They had retired into her father's library and were talking among themselves back there. Now and then she heard a laugh. She smelled the cigar smoke. They were all back there but Major Bullock.

"How's my fire?" cried Major Bullock. "Somebody tend to the fire!" he called toward the kitchen. "Important time like this, you can't do without a fire, can you?" But he kept his own watch on the doorway leading from the hall, and looked eagerly to see each one who came in.

Old Mrs. Pease kept a watch on the front walk through the parlor curtains, making herself at home. "Why, here comes Tommy," she said now. She might have been entertaining a notion of running him away, as she might have to run those Texas children if they played too near the house.

The caller entered the room without the benefit of Miss Adele, walking with a spring on the balls of his feet, striking his cane from side to side in a lordly way. He was Tom Farris, Mount Salus's blind man. Instead of going to the coffin, he went to the piano and tapped his cane on the empty piano stool.

"He's so happy," said Miss Tennyson approvingly.

He sat down, a large, very clean man with rotund, open eyes like a statue's. His fly had not been buttoned up quite straight. Laurel thought he had never been in the house before except to tune the piano, ages ago. He sat down on the same stool now.

"And under that cloak of modesty he wore, a fearless man! Fearless man!" Major Bullock suddenly burst into speech, standing at the foot of the coffin. "Remember the day, everybody, when Clint McKelva stood up and faced the White Caps?" The floor creaked agonizingly as he rocked back and forth on his feet and all but shouted, filling the room, perhaps the house, with his voice. "The time Clint sentenced that fellow for willful murder and the White Caps let it be known they were coming to town out of all their holes and nooks and crannies to take that man from the jail! And Clint just as quick sent out word of his own: he was going to ring that jail and Courthouse of ours with Mount Salus volunteers, and we'd be armed and ready. And the White Caps came, too—came a little bit earlier than they promised, little bit earlier than the rest of us got on hand. But Clint, Clint all by himself, he walked out on the front steps of that Courthouse and stood there and he said, 'Come right on in! The jail is upstairs, on the second floor!' "

"I don't think that was Father," Laurel said low to Tish, who had come up beside her.

Major Bullock was going irrepressibly on. " 'Come

in!' says he. 'But before you enter, you take those damn white hoods off, and every last one of you give me a look at who you are!' "

"He hadn't any use for what he called theatrics," Laurel was saying. "In the courtroom or anywhere else. He had no patience for show."

"He says, 'Back to your holes, rats!' And they were armed!" cried Major Bullock, lifting an imaginary gun in his hands.

"He's trying to make Father into something he wanted to be himself," said Laurel.

"Bless his heart," mourned Tish beside her. "Don't spoil it for Daddy."

"But I don't think it's fair *now,*" said Laurel.

"Well, that backed 'em right out of there, the whole pack, right on out of town and back into the woods they came from. Cooked their goose for a while!" declared Major Bullock. "Oh, under that cloak of modesty he wore—"

"Father really was modest," Laurel said to him.

"Honey, what do you mean? Honey, you were away. You were sitting up yonder in Chicago, drawing pictures," Major Bullock told her. "I saw him! He stood up and dared those rascals to shoot him! Baring his breast!"

"He would have thought of my mother," said Laurel. And with it came the thought: It was my mother who *might* have done that! She's the only one I know who had it in her.

"Remains a mystery to me how he ever stayed alive," said Major Bullock stiffly. He lowered the imaginary gun. His feelings had been hurt.

The mystery in how little we know of other people is no greater than the mystery of how much, Laurel thought.

"But who do you call the man, Dad?" asked Wendell, plucking at his father's sleeve.

"Shut up. Or I'll carry you on home without letting you see the rest of it."

"It's my father," Laurel said.

The little boy looked at her, and his mouth opened. She thought he disbelieved her.

The crowd of men were still at it behind the screen. "Clint's hunting a witness, some of the usual trouble, and this Negro girl says, 'It's him and me that saw it. He's a witness, and I's a got-shot witness.' "

They laughed.

" 'There's two kinds, all right,' says Clint. 'And I know which to take. She's the got-shot witness: I'll take her.' He could see the funny side to everything."

"He brought her here afterwards and kept her safe under his own roof," Laurel said under her breath to Miss Adele, who had come in from the door now; it would be too late for any more callers before the funeral. "I don't know what the funny side was."

"It was Missouri, wasn't it?" said Miss Adele.

"And listening," said Laurel, for Missouri herself was just then lit up by a shower of sparks; down on her knees before the fire, she was poking the big log.

"I always pray people won't recognize themselves in the speech of others," Miss Adele murmured. "And I don't think very often they do."

The log shifted like a sleeper in bed, and light flared all over in the room. Mr. Pitts was revealed in their midst as though by a spotlight, in the act of consulting his wristwatch.

"What's happening isn't real," Laurel said, low.

"The ending of a man's life on earth is very real indeed," Miss Adele said.

"But what people are saying."

"They're trying to say for a man that his life is over. Do you know a good way?"

Here, helpless in his own house among the people he'd known, and who'd known him, since the beginning, her father seemed to Laurel to have reached at this moment the danger point of his life.

"Did you listen to their words?" she asked.

"They're being clumsy. Often because they were thinking of you."

"They said he was a humorist. And a crusader. And an angel on the face of the earth," Laurel said.

Miss Adele, looking into the fire, smiled. "It isn't easy for them, either. And they're being egged on a little bit, you know, Laurel, by the rivalry that's going on here in the room," she said. "After all, when the Chisoms walked in on us, they thought they had their side, too—"

"Rivalry? With Father where he lies?"

"Yes, but people being what they are, Laurel."

"This is still his house. After all, they're still his guests. They're misrepresenting him—falsifying, that's what Mother would call it." Laurel might have been trying to testify now for her father's sake, as though he were in process of being put on trial in here instead of being viewed in his casket. "He never would have stood for lies being told about him. Not at any time. Not ever."

"Yes he would," said Miss Adele. "If the truth might hurt the wrong person."

"I'm his daughter. I want what people say now to be the truth."

Laurel slowly turned her back to the parlor, and stood a little apart from Miss Adele too. She let her eyes travel out over the coffin into the other room, her father's "library." The bank of greenery hid the sight of his desk. She could see only the two loaded bookcases behind it, like a pair of old, patched, velvety cloaks hung up there on the wall. The shelf-load of Gibbon stretched like a sagging sash across one of them. She had not read her father the book he'd wanted after all. The wrong book! The wrong book! She was looking at her own mistake, and its long shadow reaching back to join the others.

"The least anybody can do for him is *remember* right," she said.

"I believe to my soul it's the most, too," said Miss

Adele. And then warningly, "*Polly—*"

Fay at that moment burst from the hall into the parlor. She glistened in black satin. Eyes straight ahead, she came running a path through all of them toward the coffin.

Miss Adele, with a light quick move from behind her, pulled Laurel out of the way.

"No. Stop—stop her," Laurel said.

Fay brought herself short and hung over the pillow. "Oh, he looks so good with those mean old sandbags taken away and that mean old bandage pulled off of his eye!" she said fiercely.

"She's wasting no time, she's fixing to break aloose right now," said Mrs. Chisom. "Didn't even stop to speak to me."

Fay cried out, and looked around.

Sis stood up, enormous, and said, "Here I am, Wanda Fay. Cry on me."

Laurel closed her eyes, in the recognition of what had made the Chisoms seem familiar to her. They might have come out of that night in the hospital waiting room—out of all times of trouble, past or future—the great, interrelated family of those who never know the meaning of what has happened to them.

"Get back!—Who told *them* to come?" cried Fay.

"I did!" said Major Bullock, his face nothing but delight. "Found 'em without a bit of trouble! Clint scribbled 'em all down for me in the office, day before he left for New Orleans."

But Fay showed him her back. She leaned forward over the coffin. "Oh, hon, get up, get out of there," she said.

"Stop her," Laurel said to the room.

"There now," said Miss Tennyson to all of them around the coffin.

"Can't you hear me, hon?" called Fay.

"She's cracking," said Mrs. Chisom. "Just like me. Poor little Wanda Fay."

"Oh, Judge, how could you be so unfair to me?" Fay cried, while Mr. Pitts emerged from behind the greens and poised his hand on the lid. "Oh, Judge, how could you go off and leave me this way? Why did you want to treat me so unfair?"

"I can tell you're going to be a little soldier," Major Bullock said, marching to Fay's side.

"Wanda Fay *needed* that husband of hers. That's why he ought to lived. He was a care, took all her time, but you'd go through it again, wouldn't you, honey?" asked Mrs. Chisom, pulling herself to her feet. She put out her arms, walking heavily toward her daughter. "If you could have your husband back this minute."

"No," Laurel whispered.

Fay cried into the coffin, "Judge! You cheated on me!"

"Just tell him goodbye, sugar," said Major Bullock as he tried to put his arm around her shoulders, staggering a little. "That's best, just plant him a kiss—"

Fay struck out with her hands, hitting at Major Bullock and Mr. Pitts and Sis, fighting her mother, too, for a moment. She showed her claws at Laurel, and broke from the preacher's last-minute arms and threw herself forward across the coffin onto the pillow, driving her lips without aim against the face under hers. She was dragged back into the library, screaming, by Miss Tennyson Bullock, out of sight behind the bank of greenery. Judge McKelva's smoking chair lay behind them, overturned.

Laurel stood gazing down at the unchanged face of the dead, while Mrs. Chisom's voice came through the sounds of confusion in the library.

"Like mother, like daughter. Though when I had to give up her dad, they couldn't hold me half so easy. I tore up the whole house, I did."

"Where's the doctor? In hiding?" old Mrs. Pease was saying.

"She'll get over it," said Dr. Woodson. All the men except for old Tom Farris, who sat just waiting, and Major Bullock following after Fay, had withdrawn to a huddle in the hall.

"Give me those little hands," Major Bullock's voice came from the library.

"She bites." Fay's sister.

"And no wonder. It's hard to be told to give up goodness itself." Major Bullock.

Hearing his voice disembodied, Laurel realized he was drunk.

"Then why was he so *bad?*" screamed Fay. "Why did he do me so *bad?*"

"Don't cry! I'll shoot the bad man for you. Where is the bad man?" came the thin pipe of Wendell. "If you don't cry!"

"You *can't* shoot him," said Sis. "Because I say so, that's why."

"Shake her," said Mrs. Chisom's appreciative voice.

"There's no telling when she last had a decent home-cooked meal with honest vegetables," said Miss Tennyson Bullock. "That goes a long way toward explaining everything. Now, this will be just a little slap."

In the moment of silence that came after that, Laurel looked at her father for the last time, when there was only herself to see him like this. Mr. Pitts had achieved one illusion, that danger to his lived life was still alive; now there was no longer that.

"He loved my mother," Laurel spoke into the quiet.

She lifted up her head: Tish was coming to stand beside her, and old Tom Farris had remained in attendance at the back of the room. Mr. Pitts had been waiting them out in the greenery. As he stepped forward and put his strength to his task, Tish very gently winked at Laurel, and helped her to give up bearing the weight of that lid, to let it come down.

Then Mr. Pitts, as if he propelled it by using the simple power of immunity, moved through their ranks with the coffin and went first; it had been piled over with flowers in the blink of an eye. Last of all came

Miss Adele: she must have been there all the time, in the righted smoking chair, with her drawn forehead against its old brown wing.

Laurel, Miss Adele, and Missouri walked out together and watched it go. Children at play and a barking dog watched it come out, then watched the people come out behind it. Two children sat on the roof of a truck to wave at Wendell, with their hands full. They had picked the Silver Bells.

Mount Salus Presbyterian Church had been built by McKelvas, who had given it the steepest steps in town to make it as high as the Courthouse it was facing. From her place in the family pew, Laurel heard the seven members of the Bar, or their younger sons, and Bubba Chisom in his windbreaker bringing up the thundering weight of Judge McKelva in his coffin. She heard them blundering.

"Heavenly Father, may this serve to remind us that we have each and every one of us been fearfully and wonderfully made," Dr. Bolt said over the coffin, head bowed. But was that not Judge McKelva's table blessing? They were the last words Laurel heard. She watched him perform the service, but what he was saying might have been as silent as the movements of the handkerchief he passed over and over again across his forehead, and down his cheeks, and around.

Everybody remained seated while the family—the

family was Laurel, Fay, and the Bullocks—walked
back up the aisle first, behind the casket. Laurel saw
that there had not been room enough in the church for
everybody who had come. All around the walls, people
were standing; they darkened the colored glass of the
windows. Black Mount Salus had come too, and the
black had dressed themselves in black.

All of them poured down the steps together. The
casket preceded them.

"He'll touch down where He took off from," said
Miss Verna Longmeier, at the bottom. "Split it right
down the middle." Her hands ripped a seam for them:
"The Mount of Olives." Triumphantly, she set off the
other way.

There was a ringing for each car as it struck its
wheels on the cattleguard and rode up into the cemetery. The procession passed between ironwork gates
whose kneeling angels and looping vines shone black
as licorice. The top of the hill ahead was crowded with
winged angels and life-sized effigies of bygone citizens
in old-fashioned dress, standing as if by count among
the columns and shafts and conifers like a familiar set
of passengers collected on deck of a ship, on which
they all knew each other—bona-fide members of a
small local excursion, embarked on a voyage that is
always returning in dreams.

"I'm glad the big camellia will be in bloom," said

Laurel. She felt her gloved hand pressed in that of Miss Tennyson, as Fay said from her other side:

"How could the biggest fool think I was going to bury my husband with his old wife? He's going in the new part."

Laurel's eye travelled among the urns that marked the graves of the McKelvas and saw the favorite camellia of her father's, the old-fashioned *Chandlerii Elegans,* that he had planted on her mother's grave—now big as a pony, saddled with unplucked bloom living and dead, standing on a fading carpet of its own flowers.

Laurel would hardly have thought of Mount Salus Cemetery as having a "new part." It was like being driven to the other side of the moon. The procession stopped. The rest of the way was too rough, as Laurel now saw, for anything except a hearse. They got out onto the grass and clay of the petered-out road. The pick-up truck had pulled up right behind the family's car, nearly touching it with the tin sign on its bumper. "Do Unto Others Before They Do Unto You."

"What're we here for?" asked Wendell, his voice in the open air carrying though light as thistledown.

"Wendell Chisom, they've got to finish what they started, haven't they? I told you you was going to be sorry you ever begged," said Sis.

They struck out across the field. There were already a few dozen graves here, dotted uniformly with indestructible plastic Christmas poinsettias.

"Now, is everybody finding the right place?" called Miss Tennyson, her eyes skimming the crowd that went walking over the young grass. "Somebody help old Tom Farris get where he's going!"

An awning marked the site; it appeared to be the farthest one in the cemetery. As they proceeded there, black wings thudded in sudden unison, and a flock of birds flew up as they might from a ploughed field, still shaped like it, like an old map that still served new territory, and wrinkled away in the air.

Mr. Pitts waited, one more time; he stood under the awning. The family took their assigned seats. Laurel had Fay on her right, sitting with a black-gloved hand held tenderly to her cheek. The coffin, fixed in suspension over the opened grave, was on a level with their eyes now.

Miss Tennyson, still on Laurel's left, murmured close to her ear, "Look behind you. The high school band. They better be here! Clint gave 'em those horns they're sporting, gave 'em the uniforms to march in. Somebody pass 'em the word to perk up. *Of course* they're not going to get to play!"

Under Mr. Pitts' awning Laurel could smell the fieriness of flowers restored to the open air and the rawness of the clay in the opened grave. Their chairs were set on the odorless, pistachio-green of Mr. Pitts' portable grass. It could still respond, everything must respond, to some vibration underfoot: this new part of the cemetery was the very shore of the new interstate highway.

Dr. Bolt assumed position and pronounced the words. Again Laurel failed to hear what came from his lips. She might not even have heard the high school band. Sounds from the highway rolled in upon her with the rise and fall of eternal ocean waves. They were as deafening as grief. Windshields flashed into her eyes like lights through tears. Beside her, then, Fay's black hand slid from her cheek to pat her hair into place—it was over.

"I want to tell you, Laurel, what a beautiful funeral it was," said Dot Daggett, immediately after Dr. Bolt had gone down the line shaking hands with the family, and they'd all risen. "I saw everybody I know and everybody I used to know. It was old Mount Salus personified." Dot looked up at Laurel out of her old movie-actress eyes. Kissing her hand to the others, she told them goodbye, cutting Miss Tennyson Bullock.

The members of the high school band were the first to break loose. They tore across the grass, all red and gold, back to their waiting jalopy. Wendell ran at their heels. In the road he found his truck. He climbed into the back of it and threw himself down on the floor and lay flat.

The rest of the company moved at a slower pace. "Somebody mind out for old Tom Farris!" called Miss

Tennyson. Laurel, letting them go ahead, walked into the waiting arms of Missouri.

In the wake of their footsteps, the birds settled again. Down on the ground, they were starlings, all on the waddle, pushing with the yellow bills of spring.

❀ *4*

IN THE PARLOR, the fire had mercifully died out. Missouri and Miss Tennyson got all the chairs back into place in the two rooms here and the dining room, and the crowd of bridesmaids had succeeded among them in winding the clock on the mantel and setting the hands to the time—only ten minutes past noon—and starting the pendulum.

Miss Tennyson Bullock, from the dining room, gave out the great groan she always gave when a dish had been made exactly right; it was her own chicken mousse. She invited them in.

Fay stared at the spread table, where Miss Tennyson, Miss Adele, Tish, and some of the other bridesmaids were setting plates and platters around. Missouri, back in her apron but with cemetery clay sticking to her heels, was bringing in the coffee urn. Missouri looked at her own reflection in the shield of its side and lifted her smiling face to Laurel.

"Now!" she said softly. "The house looking like it used to look! Like it used to look!"

"So you see? Here's the Virginia ham!" said the minister's wife to Laurel, as if everything had turned out all right: she offered her a little red rag of it on a Ritz cracker. Then she scampered away to her husband.

As soon as she was out of the house, Major Bullock carried in the silver tray heavy with some bottles and a pitcher and a circle of silver cups and tall glasses.

"Wanda Fay, you got enough stuff in sight to last one lone woman forever," said Bubba Chisom, both his hands around a ham sandwich.

"I think things have gone off real well," said Fay.

"Poor little girl!" Major Bullock said. As he offered her one of the silver cups with whiskey and water in it— she let him go on holding it—he said again, "Poor little girl. I reckon you know you *get* the house and everything in it you want. And Laurel having her own good place in Chicago, she'll be compensated as equally as we know how—"

"Oh, foot," said old Mrs. Pease.

"I sure do know whose house this is," said Fay. "But maybe it's something a few other people are going to have to learn."

Major Bullock lifted the cup he'd offered to her and drank it himself.

"Well, you've done fine so far, Wanda Fay," said old Mrs. Chisom. "I was proud of you today. And proud for you. That coffin made me wish I could have taken it right away from him and given it to Roscoe."

"Thank you," said Fay. "It was no bargain, and I think that showed."

"Still, I did the best *I* could. And I feel like Roscoe sits up there knowing it now," said Mrs. Chisom. "And what more could you ask."

"You drew a large crowd, too," said Sis. "Without even having to count those Negroes."

"I was satisfied with it," said Fay.

"For the first minute, you didn't act all that glad to see *us*," said Sis. "Or was I dreaming?"

"Now, be sisters," warned old Mrs. Chisom. "And I'm glad you broke down *when you did,* Wanda Fay," she went on, wagging her finger. "There's a time and a place for everything. You try begging for sympathy later on, when folks has gone back about their business, and they don't appreciate your tears then. It just tries their nerves."

"Wanda Fay, I'm sorry I can't fool around here no longer," said Bubba Chisom, handing her his empty plate. "A wrecking concern hasn't got all that time to spare, not with all we got to do in Madrid."

"Come on, then," said Sis, who had pushed herself to her feet again. "Let's get going before the children commence to fighting and Wendell starts giving trouble again. Wendell Chisom," she said to the little boy, "you can take this home to your mother: this is the first and last time you're ever going to be carried to a funeral in any charge of me." She took Laurel's hand and shook it. "We thought a heap of your old dad, even if he couldn't stay on earth long enough for us to get to know him. Whatever he was, we always knew he was just plain *folks*."

Through the open front door could be seen the old grandfather already outside with his hat on, walking around looking at the trees. The pecan tree there was filled with budding leaves like green bees spaced out in a hive of light. There was something bright as well in the old man's hatband—the other half of his round-trip ticket from Bigbee.

"Wanda Fay," said Mrs. Chisom, "let me ask you this: who're you ever going to get to put in this house besides you?"

"What are you hinting at?" said Fay with a dark look.

"Tell you one thing, there's room for the whole nation of *us* here," Mrs. Chisom said, and stepping back into the hall she looked up the white-railed stairway. "In case we ever took a notion to move back to Mississippi." She went outside and they heard her stepping along the front porch. "It'd make a good boarding house, if you could get your mother to come cook for 'em."

"Great Day in the Morning!" exclaimed Miss Tennyson Bullock.

"Mama," said Fay, "you know what? I've got a good mind this minute to jump in with you. And ride home with my folks to Texas." Her chin was trembling as she named it. "Hear?"

"For how long do you mean to stay?" asked Mrs. Chisom, coming to face her.

"Just long enough."

"You going to rush into a trip right now?" Major Bullock asked, going to her other side.

"Major Bullock," she said, "I think when a person can see a free ride one way, the decision is made for them. And it just so happens I haven't unpacked my suitcase."

"I haven't heard your excuse for going yet," said Sis. "Have you got one?"

"I'd just like to see somebody that can talk my language, that's my excuse. Where's DeWitt?" Fay demanded. "You didn't bring him."

"DeWitt? He's still in Madrid. He's been in a sull ever since you married Judge McKelva and didn't send him a special engraved invitation to the wedding," said Bubba.

Fay gave them a tight smile.

Mrs. Chisom said, "I said, 'DeWitt, now! You're a brother just the same as Bubba is—and Roscoe was— and it's your place to get up out of that sull and come on with us to the funeral. You can take the wheel in Lake Charles.' But DeWitt is DeWitt, he expects his feelings to be considered."

"He speaks my language," said Fay. "I've got a heap to tell DeWitt."

"You may have to stand out in front of his house and holler it, if you do," said Bubba. "He's got folks' appliances stacked over ever' blooming inch of space. You can't hardly get in across those vacuum cleaners and power motors and bathroom heaters and old window fans, and not a one of 'em running. Hasn't fixed a one. He can't hardly get out of the house and you can't get in."

"I'll scare him out of that sull," said Fay.

"I think that's just what he's waiting for, myself," said Sis. "I wouldn't give him the satisfaction, if it was me."

Fay cried, "I don't even mind standing up in the back and riding with the children!" She whirled and ran upstairs.

"You'll wind up riding on my lap," said her mother. "I know you." She put her hand out and stopped a tray going by. "I wouldn't mind taking some of that ham along, though," she told Tish. "If it's just going begging."

Laurel followed Fay upstairs and stood in the bedroom door while Fay stuffed her toilet things into the already crammed suitcase.

"Fay, I wanted you to know what day I'll be leaving," she said. "So there'll be no danger of us running into each other."

"That suits me dandy."

"I'm giving myself three days. And I'll leave Monday on the three o'clock flight from Jackson. I'll be out of the house around noon."

"All right, then." Fay slammed her suitcase shut. "You just try and be as good as your word.—I'm coming, Mama! Don't you-all go off and leave me!" she yelled over Laurel's head.

"Fay, I wanted to ask you something, too," Laurel said. "What made you tell me what you did about your family? The time we talked, in the Hibiscus."

"What did I say?" Fay challenged her.

"You said you had nobody—no family. You lied about your family."

"If I did, that's what everybody else does," said Fay. "Why shouldn't I?"

"Not lie that they're dead."

"It's better than some lies I've heard around here!" cried Fay. She struggled to lift her suitcase, and Laurel, as if she'd just seen her in the deepest trouble, moved instinctively to help her. But Fay pushed on past her, dragging it, and hobbled in front of her, bumping her load a step ahead of her down the stairs. She had changed into her green shoes.

"I believe a few days with your own family would do you good," Miss Tennyson Bullock said. In the dining room, all of them were waiting on their feet. "Eating a lot of fresh vegetables, and so forth."

"Well, at least my family's not hypocrites," said Fay. "If they didn't want me, they'd tell me to my face."

"When you coming back?" asked Major Bullock, swaying a little.

"When I get ready."

The clock struck for half-past twelve.

"Oh, how I hate that old striking clock!" cried Fay. "It's the first thing I'm going to get rid of."

They were taking old Mr. Chisom as far as the bus station, to be sure he found it.

"You got a lot of fat squirrels going to waste here," the old man said, bending down to Laurel, and she was unprepared for it when he kissed her goodbye.

At last they were in the truck, rolling down the driveway to the street.

"Poor little woman. Got a bigger load than she knows yet how to carry by herself," said Major Bullock, waving.

Wendell was the only Chisom visible now, standing at the very back of the truck. He pulled one of his guns out of the holster and rode off shooting it at them. No noise came but his own thin, wistful voice.

"Pow! Pow! Pow!"

The few who were left walked back into the house. The silver tray on the hall table held a heap of calling cards, as though someone had tried to build a little house with them. Beside it lay a candy box with the picture of a pretty girl on the dusty lid.

"Old Mr. Chisom gave me all those pecans he

brought," said Laurel, sighing. "I don't know why. Then he kissed me when he left."

"I believe he thought you must be Fay," said Miss Adele gently.

"I'm making myself a little toddy," said Miss Tennyson, adding sugar to something in a glass. "Do you know, Laurel, who was coming to my mind the whole blessed way through? *Becky!*"

"Of course," said Miss Adele.

"And all I did was thank my stars she wasn't here. Child, I'm glad your mother didn't have to live through that. I'm glad it was you."

"Foot! I'm mad at you for not getting the house," old Mrs. Pease told Laurel. "After all, I'm the one that's got to go on living next door." She went home.

The others were leaving too. "Rupert, I could brain you for roping in those Chisoms," said Miss Tennyson, as the Major took her by the arm.

"I thought they'd be the answer to her prayers, poor little woman. And Clint jotted the list of 'em down for me just the day he took off for New Orleans. In case she needed 'em."

"And she did," said Miss Adele.

"I still can't believe it!" the Major loudly said, as the Bullocks helped each other toward the old Chrysler. "Can't believe we've all come off and left him in the ground!"

"Rupert," said Miss Tennyson, "now listen to me. Believe it. Now you get busy and believe it. Do you hear what I say? Poor Clinton's in Heaven right now."

Miss Adele took a step toward the kitchen, and then Missouri clinked some glasses back there. Miss Adele lifted her empty hands for a moment, and dropped them.

Laurel touched her own to one of hers, and watched her go.

Three

I

LAUREL, KNEELING, worked among the iris that still held a ragged line along the back of the house up to the kitchen door. She'd found the dark-blue slacks and the blue cardigan in her suitcase—she'd packed them as automatically as she'd packed her sketchbook. She felt the spring sun gently stinging the back of her neck and she listened to other people talk. Her callers sat behind her and over to the side, in the open sunshine.

"Well, we got her out of the house," Miss Tennyson Bullock said. "Fay's gone!"

"Don't brag too soon," said old Mrs. Pease.

These four elderly ladies were all at home in the McKelva backyard. Cardinals, flying down from low branches of the dogwood tree, were feeding here and there at the ladies' crossed feet. At the top of the tree, a mockingbird stood silent over them like a sentinel.

"I used to waste good time feeling sorry for Clint. But he's in Heaven now. And if she's in Texas, I can just sit here in sunshine and be glad for *our* sakes," Miss Tennyson said. She had the ancient deck chair, which engulfed her like a hammock. "Of course, Major daily expects her back."

"Oh, but not to stay, do you think? In Mount Salus without a husband?" asked Mrs. Bolt, the minister's wife. She promptly reassured herself. "No, she won't last long. She'll go away."

"I wouldn't count on it if I were you," said old Mrs. Pease. "You got a peep at her origins."

"Ask yourself what other roof than this she'd rather have over her head, and you've got your answer," said Miss Tennyson.

"What did she do with herself while he was *here?*" exclaimed Mrs. Bolt.

"Nothing but sit-and-eat," said Miss Tennyson. "And keep straight on looking like a sparrow."

"She had to eat. Had nothing else to do to occupy her hands," said Mrs. Pease, holding up a perfectly enormous afghan she was knitting as if by the porcelain light of the dogwood tree.

"Oh, surely you know she was occupied enough with this great big house to care for." Miss Adele tilted up her face at it. The faint note of mockery that belonged in her voice had come back today.

"The house was not exactly a *sight*. Yes it was," said Miss Tennyson. "The way they set off and left it to come back to—I won't describe the way Adele and I found it."

"Their bed wasn't made," suggested the minister's wife.

"Well, if she made him happy. You've never caught me guilty yet of saying any more than that," said Miss Tennyson.

The wild phlox was blue as a lake behind Miss Adele

Courtland as she said, "Oh, indeed he doted on her."

"Doted. You've hit on it. That's the word," said Miss Tennyson.

Laurel went on pulling weeds. Her mother's voice came back with each weed she reached for, and its name with it. "Ironweed." "Just chickweed." "Here comes that miserable old vine!"

"It couldn't be for her bridge game, if dote he did. Beggar-my-neighbor was more in her line of accomplishment," said old Mrs. Pease grimly.

"Oh, he doted on her, exactly like a man will. I'd only wish to ask your precious father one question, if I could have him back just long enough for that, Laurel," said Miss Tennyson, and with effort she leaned forward and asked it hoarsely: "What happened to his judgment?"

"He wasn't as old as all that," agreed Mrs. Pease. "I'm older. By a trifle."

"A man can feel compunction for a child like Fay and still not have to carry it that far," said Miss Tennyson. She called, "Laurel, do you know that when he brought her here to your house, she had very little idea of how to separate an egg?"

"And neither did he," said Miss Adele.

" 'Frying pan' was the one name she could give you of all the things your mother had in that kitchen, Laurel. Things like that get over town in a hurry, you know. I hate to tell you the upshot," said Miss Tennyson, "but on Sundays, when no power on earth could bring Missouri, they walked from church and took their Sunday dinner in the Iona Hotel, in that dining room."

On top of the tree, the mockingbird threw out his chest and let fall a cascade of song.

"Oh, it's been the most saddening exhibition within my memory," said old Mrs. Pease, crablike over her wool.

"Major and I just happen to walk that way too, when we go home from church. Sunday after Sunday we saw 'em through the dirty plate-glass window," said Miss Tennyson. "Billing and cooing. No tablecloth."

"A good thing you reminded me!" said Mrs. Bolt. "My husband hasn't yet rehearsed his Sunday sermon to me, and he's got just today and tomorrow." She took her leave.

"Shocked her, but that service of her husband's wasn't up to Clinton, either," said Miss Tennyson, settling back in the big old chair. "At the time, I didn't object—the catch came in thinking it over later."

"The whole day left something to be desired, if you want to hear me come right out with it," said old Mrs. Pease.

"Go ahead. I know you're blaming Major," said Miss Tennyson. "Why he had to get so carried away as to round up those Chisoms, I'll never know, myself. He said they were nothing but just good old Anglo-Saxons. But I said—"

"You can't curb a Baptist," Mrs. Pease said. "Let

them in and you can't keep 'em down, when somebody dies. When the whole bunch of Chisoms got to going in concert, I thought the only safe way to get through the business alive was not say a word, just sit as still as a mouse."

"I, though, consider that the Chisoms did every bit as well as we did," said Miss Adele. "If we're going to dare mention behavior."

"Adele has the schoolteacher's low opinion of everybody," said Miss Tennyson.

"It's true they were a trifle more inelegant," said Miss Adele. "But only a trifle."

"The pitiful thing was, Fay didn't know any better than the rest of 'em. She just supposed she did," said Miss Tennyson.

"Did you hear her snub her sister? Refused to cry on her," said old Mrs. Pease.

"Well, we all knew exactly what the sort of thing *was* that Fay'd be good for," said Miss Tennyson. "Didn't make it go any quicker when it came. That slap I gave her took the starch out of *me*."

"Strangely enough," said Miss Adele, "I think that carrying-on was Fay's idea of giving a sad occasion its due. She was rising to it, splendidly.—By her lights!" she interrupted herself before the others could do it for her. "She wanted nothing but the best for her husband's funeral, only the most expensive casket, the most choice cemetery plot—"

"Choice! It looked right out on the Interstate! Those

horrible trucks made so much whine, not a thing Dr. Bolt was saying could be heard. Even from our good seats," said Miss Tennyson.

"—and," continued Miss Adele, "the most broken-hearted, most distraught behavior she could manage on the part of the widow."

Singing over her words, the mockingbird poured out his voice without stopping.

"I could have broken her neck," said Miss Tennyson.

"Well, you couldn't expect her to stop being a Baptist," said old Mrs. Pease.

"Well, of course I'm a Baptist," said Miss Adele, the dimple coming into her cheek.

"Adele, you didn't care for Fay's behavior any more than the rest of us did," said Miss Tennyson.

"I saw you have to sit down," said old Mrs. Pease shrewdly.

"I give myself as bad a mark as anybody. Never fear," said Miss Adele.

"Well, I'm not ashamed of anything *I* did," said Miss Tennyson. "And I felt still more ashamed for Fay when she upped and told us goodbye and went off with the rest of the Chisoms. I reckon she thought we might not let her go. But we didn't beg her any too hard to stay, did we?" Miss Tennyson sank back deeper into the old chair.

"As a matter of fact," said Miss Adele, "Fay stuck to her guns longer than the rest of us, the ones who knew Judge McKelva better, and knew everything better.

Major Bullock got outright tipsy, and everybody that opened their mouths said as near the wrong thing as they could possibly manage."

"Adele! You just dearly love to punish yourself. You *hate* what you're saying, just as much as we do," declared Miss Tennyson.

"But I believe it."

"Well, I'm going right on blaming the Chisoms," said old Mrs. Pease. "They ought to have stayed home in the first place. All of 'em."

"I further believe Fay thought she was rising in the estimation of Mount Salus, there in front of all his life-long friends," said Miss Adele. "And on what she thought was the prime occasion for doing it."

"Well, she needed somebody to tell her how to act," said Miss Tennyson flatly.

"I gathered from the evidence we were given that Fay was emulating her own mother," said Miss Adele, while the mockingbird sang.

"Why, Fay declared right in front of old Mrs. Chisom and all that she wished her mother hadn't come!" said Miss Tennyson.

"Nevertheless, that's who she emulated," said Miss Adele. "We can't find fault with doing that, can we, Laurel?"

Laurel, who had worked her way as far as the kitchen door, sat on the back step and gazed at the ladies, all four.

"I got the notion if Fay hadn't turned around quick,

they might've just settled in here with her," said old Mrs. Pease. "When old Mrs. What's-her-name stepped off the reach of the front porch, I had an anxious moment, I can tell you."

"Are we all going to have to feel sorry for her?" asked Miss Tennyson.

"If there's nothing else to do, there's no help for it," said Miss Adele. "Is there, Laurel?"

"Well, answer!" exclaimed Miss Tennyson. "Are you prepared now to pity her, Laurel?"

"Cat's got her tongue," said old Mrs. Pease.

"I hope I never see her again," said Laurel.

"There, girlie, you got it out," said Miss Tennyson. "She's a trial to us all and nothing else. Why don't you stay on here, and help us with her?"

"Why not indeed?" said Miss Adele. "Laurel has no other life."

"Of course I must get back to work," said Laurel.

"Back to work." Miss Tennyson pointed her finger at Laurel and told the others, "That girl's had more now than she can say grace over. And she's going back to that life of labor when she could just as easily give it up. Clint's left her a grand hunk of money."

"Once you leave after this, you'll always come back as a visitor," Mrs. Pease warned Laurel. "Feel free, of course—but it was always my opinion that people don't really want visitors."

"I mean it. Why track back up to the North Pole?"

asked Miss Tennyson. "Who's going to kill you if you don't draw those pictures? As I was saying to Tish, 'Tish, if Laurel would stay home and Adele would retire, we could have as tough a bridge foursome as we had when Becky was playing.'"

"Are you figuring on running me out, then? Or what?" asked old Mrs. Pease, who had tottered to her feet.

"No, play on as you're playing now," said Miss Adele, smiling. "Nate's adorable French wife in New Orleans would agree with Laurel perfectly: there's not enough Mount Salus has to *offer* a brilliant mind."

"There!" exclaimed Miss Tennyson. "I'd begun to despair that we could ever make Laurel McKelva laugh on this trip at all."

"I've got my passage," Laurel said. "The afternoon flight from Jackson on Monday."

"And she'll make it, too. Oh, Laurel can do anything. If it's been made hard enough for her," said Miss Adele. "Of *course* she can give up Mount Salus and say goodbye to this house and to us, and the past, and go on back to Chicago day after tomorrow, flying a jet. And take up one more time where she left off."

Laurel stood up and kissed the mischievous, wrinkled cheek.

"Laurel, look yonder. You still might change your mind if you could see the roses bloom, see Becky's Climber come out," said Miss Tennyson softly.

"I can imagine it, in Chicago."

"But you can't smell it," Miss Tennyson argued.

All of them wandered toward the rose bed, where every hybrid tea stood low with branches cut staggered. They were hiding themselves in an opalescent growth of leaf. Behind them—Laurel took a few steps farther —the climbers rose: Mermaid, solid as a thicket, on the Pease side, and Banksia in its first feathery bloom on the Courtland side, and between them the width of bare fence where Becky's Climber belonged. Judge McKelva had recalled himself at Becky's Climber.

("I'd give a pretty to know what exactly that rose is!" Laurel's mother would say every spring when it opened its first translucent flowers of the true rose color. "It's an old one, with an old fragrance, and has every right to its own name, but nobody in Mount Salus is interested in giving it to me. All I had to do was uncover it and give it the room it asked for. Look at it! It's on its own roots, of course, utterly strong. That old root there may be a hundred years old!"

"Or older," Judge McKelva had said, giving her, from the deck chair, his saturnine smile. "Strong as an old apple tree.")

Sienna-bright leaves and thorns like spurts of match-flame had pierced through the severely cut-back trunk. If it didn't bloom this year, it would next: "That's how gardeners must learn to look at it," her mother would say.

Memory returned like spring, Laurel thought. Memory had the character of spring. In some cases, it was the old wood that did the blooming.

"So we've settled Laurel. But has anybody but Tennyson settled Fay? I don't see how we can think so," said Miss Adele, with the excruciated dimple making a shadow in her cheek. "When we really lack the first idea of knowing what to do with Clinton's little minx, whom he's left on our hands in such utter disregard for our feelings." She was doing her best, getting back into her form today.

"Short of crowning her over the head with a good solid piece of something," agreed Miss Tennyson. "She'll live forever and a day. She'll be right here when we're gone. Why do all the men think they need to *protect* her?"

"Major just slobbers over her," old Mrs. Pease agreed.

"But he wasn't the *prime* idiot. Wouldn't Clint be amazed if he suddenly had ears again and could hear us right now?" said Miss Tennyson with relish. "You know, I marvel at men."

"Laurel is who should have saved him from that nonsense. Laurel shouldn't have married a naval officer in wartime. Laurel should have stayed home after Becky died. He needed him somebody *in* that house, girl," said old Mrs. Pease.

"But that didn't have to mean Fay," said Miss Tennyson. "Drat her!"

"She's never done anybody any harm," Miss Adele remarked. "Rather, she gave a lonely old man something to live for."

"I'd rather not consider how," interrupted Miss Tennyson primly.

"We just resent her, poor little waif," said Miss Adele. "And she can't help but know it. She's got more resentment than we have. Resentment *born*."

"If I'd just known Clint was casting around for somebody to take Becky's place, I could've found him one a whole lot better than Fay. And right here in Mount Salus," Miss Tennyson was stung to say. "I could name one now that would have *leaped*—"

"He didn't find Becky in Mount Salus," Miss Adele reminded them, silencing all but the mockingbird.

"And of course that's one of the peculiarities Laurel inherited from *him*. She didn't look at home to find Philip Hand," said Miss Tennyson.

Laurel stood up.

"Laurel's ready for us to go," said Miss Adele, rising herself. "We've kept her out of the house long enough."

"No, don't ask us in, we'll leave you to struggle through the rest without us," said Miss Tennyson indulgently. She waved her way out toward the street. Old Mrs. Pease walked slowly away, folding her afghan, and turned through the gate that opened into her untrespassed garden.

As Laurel walked with Miss Adele toward her own opening in the hedge, there could be heard a softer sound than the singing from the dogwood tree. It was rhythmic but faint, as from the shaking of a tambourine.

"Little mischiefs! Will you look at them showing off," said Miss Adele.

A cardinal took his dipping flight into the fig tree and brushed wings with a bird-frightener, and it crashed faintly. Another cardinal followed, then a small band of them. Those thin shimmering discs were polished, rain-bright, and the redbirds, all rival cocks, were flying at their tantalizing reflections. At the tiny crash the birds would cut a figure in the air and tilt in again, then again.

"Oh, it's a game, isn't it, nothing but a game!" Miss Adele said, stepping gracefully into her own backyard.

❈ *2*

LAUREL faced the library. This was where, after his retirement and marriage, her father had moved everything he wanted around him from his office in the Mount Salus Bank Building on the Square.

Perhaps a crowded room, whatever is added, always looks the same. One wall was exactly the same. Above one bookcase hung her father's stick-framed map of the county—he had known every mile; above the other hung the portraits of his father and grandfather, the Confederate general and missionary to China, as alike as two peaches, painted by the same industrious hand on boards too heavy to hang straight, but hanging side by side: the four eyebrows had been identically outlined in the shape of little hand-saws placed over the eyes, teeth down, then filled in with lamp-black.

She saw at once that nothing had happened to the books. *Flush Times in Alabama and Mississippi,* the title running catercornered in gold across its narrow green spine, was in exactly the same place as ever, next to Tennyson's Poetical Works, Illustrated, and that next to Hogg's *Confessions of a Justified Sinner.* She ran her finger in a loving track across *Eric Brighteyes* and *Jane Eyre, The Last Days of Pompeii* and *Carry On, Jeeves.* Shoulder to shoulder, they had long since made their own family. For every book here she had heard their voices, father's and mother's. And perhaps it didn't matter to them, not always, what they read aloud; it was the breath of life flowing between them, and the words of the moment riding on it that held them in delight. Between some two people every word is beautiful, or might as well be beautiful. In the other bookcase, which stood a little lower—maybe because of Webster's *Un-abridged* and the McKelva family Bible, twin weights, lying on top—there was the Dickens all in a set, a shelf and a half full, old crimson bindings scorched and frayed and hanging in strips. *Nicholas Nickleby* was the volume without any back at all. It was the Gibbon below it, that had *not* been through fire, whose backs had come to be the color of ashes. And Gibbon was not sacrosanct: *The Adventures of Sherlock Holmes* looked out from between two volumes. Laurel dusted all of them, and set them back straight in the same order.

The library was a little darker now that one of the two windows that looked out on the Courtland side of the house was covered by Judge McKelva's office cabinet. This was jammed with lawbooks and journals, more dictionaries, his Claiborne's *Mississippi* and his Mississippi Code. Books, folders, file boxes were shelved with markers and tapes hanging out. Along the cabinet top his telescope was propped extended, like a small brass cannon.

Laurel slid back the glass doors and began to dust and put back neatly what she came to. His papers were in an order of their own—she thought it was that of importance to unimportance. He had kept civic papers dating from the days when he was Mayor of Mount Salus, and an old dedication speech made at the opening of the new school ("These are my promises to you, all the young people I see before me: . . ."). The promises had made them important to him. There was a bursting folder of papers having to do with the Big Flood, the one that had ruined the McKelva place on the river; it was jammed with the work he had done on floods and flood control. And everybody had already forgotten all about that part of his life, his work, his *drudgery*. This town deserved him no more than Fay deserved him, she thought, her finger in the dust on what he'd written.

Laurel took her eyes away from words and stood for a moment at the window. In the backyard next door, Miss Adele was hanging something white on the clothesline. She turned as if intuitively toward the window, and raised her arm to wave. It was a beckoning sort of wave. She beckons with her pain, thought Laurel, realizing how often her father must have stood just here, resting his eyes, and looked out at her without ever seeing her.

Yet he loved them as a family. After moving into town from out in the country, the Courtlands ploughed the field behind the house, and back of that, in the pasture, kept cows. In Laurel's early memory, Mrs. Courtland had sold milk and to Judge McKelva's disturbance had had her children drink it skimmed blue so she could sell all the cream.

It was not until that night when Dr. Courtland told her, that Laurel ever heard he owed part of his medical schooling to her father. Never had Judge McKelva been well off until the last few years. He had come unexpectedly into a little oil money from a well dug in those acres of sand he still owned in the country—not a great deal, but enough, with his salary continuing for life, to retire on free of financial worry.

"*See there?*" he had written to Laurel—or rather dictated to Dot, who loved underlining his words on her typewriter. "There was never anything wrong with keeping up a little optimism over the Flood. How well would you like to knock off, invite a friend for company, and all go see England and Scotland in the spring?" The next thing she heard, he was about to marry Fay.

She'd been all around the room, and now there was the desk. It stood in the center of the room, and it had been her father's great-grandfather's, made in Edinburgh—a massive, concentrated presence, like that of a concert grand. (The neglected piano in the parlor seemed to have no presence at all.) Behind the desk yawned his leather chair, now in its proper place.

Laurel walked around to it. There used to be standing on the desk, to face him in his chair, a photograph of her mother, who had been asked to stop what she was doing and sit on the garden bench—this was the strongly severe result; and the picture was gone. That was understandable. The only photograph here now was of herself and Philip running down the steps of the Mount Salus Presbyterian Church after their wedding. Her father had given it a silver frame. (So had she. Her marriage had been of magical ease, of *ease* —of brevity and conclusion and all belonging to Chicago and not here.)

But something had been spilled on the desk. There were vermilion drops of hardened stuff on the dark wood—not sealing wax; nail polish. They made a little track toward the chair, as if Fay had walked her fingers over the desk from where she'd sat perched on its corner, doing her nails.

Laurel seated herself in her father's chair and reached for the top drawer of his desk, which she had never thought of opening in her life. It was not locked—had it ever been? The drawer rolled out almost weightless, as light as his empty cigar box, the only thing inside. She opened the drawers one after the other on both sides of the huge desk: they had been cleaned out. Someone had, after all, been here ahead of her.

Of course, his documents he had placed in the office safe; they were in Major Bullock's charge now, and his will was in Chancery court. But what of all the letters written to him—her mother's letters?

Her mother had written to him every day they were separated in their married lives; she had said so. He often went about to court, made business trips; and she, every summer since she had married him, had spent a full month in West Virginia, "up home," usually with Laurel along. Where were the letters? Put away somewhere, with her garden picture?

They weren't anywhere, because he hadn't kept them. He'd never kept them: Laurel knew it and should have known it to start with. He had dispatched all his correspondence promptly, and dropped letters as he answered them straight into the wastebasket;

Laurel had seen him do it. And when it concerned her
mother, if that was what she asked for, he *went*.

But there was nothing of her mother here for Fay to
find, or for herself to retrieve. The only traces there
were of anybody were the drops of nail varnish. Laurel
studiously went to work on them; she lifted them from
the surface of the desk and rubbed it afterwards with
wax until nothing was left to show of them, either.

That was on Saturday.

 3

"Laurel! Remember when we really *were* the bridesmaids?" Tish cried as they sat over drinks after dinner.
It was Sunday evening.

While the bridesmaids' parents still lived within a
few blocks of the McKelva house, the bridesmaids
and their husbands had mostly all built new houses
in the "new part" of Mount Salus. Their own children
were farther away still, off in college now.

Tish's youngest son was still at home. "He won't
come out, though," Tish had said. "He has company.
A girl came in through his bedroom window—to play

chess with him. That's what she said. I think she's the same one who came in through his window last night, close to eleven o'clock. I saw car lights in the driveway and went to see. They call him every minute. Girls. He's fifteen."

"And remember Mama at the wedding," Tish said now, "crying when it was over, saying to your father, 'Oh, Clint, isn't it the saddest thing?' And Judge Mac saying, 'Why, no, Tennyson, if I had thought there was anything sad to be said for it, I should have prevented it.' "

"*Prevented* it? I never saw a man enjoy a wedding more," said Gert.

"Wartime or no wartime, we had pink champagne that Judge Mac sent all the way to New Orleans for!" one of the others cried. "And a five-piece Negro band. Remember?"

"Miss Becky thought it was utter extravagance. Child-foolishness. But Judge Mac insisted on it all, a big wedding right on down the line."

"Well, Laurel was an only child."

"Mother had a superstitious streak underneath," Laurel said protectively. "She might have had a notion it was unlucky to make too much of your happiness." From her place on the chaise longue by the window, she saw lightning flickering now in the western sky, like the feathers of a bird taking a bath.

"Judge Mac laughed her out of it, then. Remember the parties we had for you!" Gert gave Laurel a lovingly derisive slap. "That was before the Old Country Club burned down, there never was another dance floor like that."

"What kind of dancer was Phil, Polly? I forget!" Tish lifted her arms as though the memory would come up and dance her away to remind her.

"Firm," said Laurel. She turned her cheek a little further away on the pillow.

"Your daddy knew how to enjoy a grand occasion as well as we did—as long as it stayed elegant, and as long as Papa didn't get too high before it was over," Tish said. "Of course, Mama should have saved all her tears for her own child's wedding." Tish was the only divorcée, as Laurel was the only widow. Tish had eloped with the captain of their high school football team.

"But Miss Becky would rather go through anything than a grand occasion," said Gert.

"I remember once—it must've been the Bar Association Meeting, or maybe when he was Mayor and they had to function at some to-do in Jackson—anyway, once Judge Mac himself bought Miss Becky a dress to wear, came home with it in a box and surprised her. Beaded crepe! Shot beads! Neck to hem, shot beads," said Tish. "Where could you have been, Laurel?"

Gert said, "He'd picked it out in New Orleans. Some *clerk* sold it to him."

Music started up from off in another room of the house. Duke Ellington.

"The young don't dance to him. They play chess to him, I suppose," Tish said aside to Laurel. "And Miss Becky said, 'Clinton, if I'd just been told in advance you were going to make me an extravagant present, I'd have asked you for a load of floor sweepings from the cottonseed-oil mill.' Can't you hear her?" Tish cried.

"She wore it, though, didn't she?" one of them asked, and Tish said, "Oh, they'd do anything for each other! Sure she wore it. And the weight she had to carry! Miss Becky told Mama in confidence that when she wasn't wearing that dress, which was nearly a hundred per cent of the time, she had to keep it in a bucket!"

The bridesmaids laughed till they cried.

"But when she wanted to justify him, she wore it! With an air. What floored me, Laurel, was him getting married again. When I saw Fay!" said Gert. "When I saw what he *had* there!"

"Mama, for his sake, asked at the beginning if she wouldn't be allowed to give some sort of little welcome for her—a sitdown tea, I believe she had in mind. And Fay said, 'Oh, please don't bother with a big wholesale reception. That kind of thing was for Becky.' Poor Judge Mac! Because except when it came to picking a wife," Tish said, smiling at Laurel, "he was a pretty worldly old sweet."

"Since when have you started laughing at them?" Laurel asked in a trembling voice. "Are they just figures from now on to make a good story?" She turned on Tish. "And you can wink over Father?"

"Polly!" Tish grabbed her. "We weren't laughing at them. They weren't funny—no more than my father and mother are! No more than all our fathers and mothers are!" She laughed again, into Laurel's face. "Aren't we grieving? We're grieving *with* you."

"I know. Of course I know it," said Laurel.

She smiled her thanks and kissed them all. She would see the bridesmaids once more. At noon tomorrow they were coming for her, all six, to drive her to her plane.

"I'm glad there's nobody else for you to lose, dear," Miss Tennyson Bullock said staunchly. She and the Major had driven over, late as it was, to tell Laurel goodbye.

"What do you mean! She's got Fay," Major Bullock protested. "Though that poor little girl's got a mighty big load on her shoulders. More'n she can bear."

"We are only given what we are able to bear," Miss Tennyson corrected him. They'd had such a long married life that she could make a pronouncement sound more military than he could, and even more legal.

Laurel hugged them both, and then said she intended to walk home.

"Walk!" "It's raining!" "Nobody ever walks in Mount Salus!" They made a fuss over letting her go. Major Bullock insisted on escorting her.

On this last night, a warm wind began to blow and

the rain fell fitfully, as though working up to some disturbance. Major Bullock shot his umbrella open and held it over Laurel in gallant fashion. He set the pace at something of a military clip.

Major Bullock lived through his friends. He lived their lives with them—up to a point, Laurel thought. While Miss Tennyson lived his. In a kind, faraway tenor, he began to hum as they went along. He seemed to have put something behind him, tonight. He was recovering his good spirits already.

> *"He rambled,*
> *He rambled,*
> *Rambled all around,*
> *In and out of town,*
> *Oh, didn't he ramble—"*

The leafing maples were bowing around the Square, and the small No U-Turn sign that hung over the cross street was swinging and turning over the wire in trapeze fashion. The Courthouse clock could not be read. In the poorly lit park, the bandstand and the Confederate statue stood in dim aureoles of rain, looking the ghosts they were, and somehow married to each other, by this time.

"He rambled till we had to cut him down," sang Major Bullock.

The house was dark among its trees.

"Fay hasn't come," said the Major. "Oh, what a shame."

"I expect we'll just miss each other," said Laurel.

"What a shame. Not to tell each other goodbye and good luck and the rest, it's too bad."

Pushing his umbrella before them, Major Bullock took her to the door and went with her inside to turn on the hall lights. His mouth knocked against hers, as though it knocked perfunctorily on a door, or on a dream—an old man's goodnight; and she saw him out, lighted his way, then shut the door on him fast.

She had seen something wrong: there was a bird in the house. It was one of the chimney swifts. It shot out of the dining room and now went arrowing up the stairwell in front of her eyes.

Laurel, still in her coat, ran through the house, turning on the lights in every room, shutting the windows against the rain, closing the doors into the hall everywhere behind her against the bird. She ran upstairs, slammed her own door, ran across the hall and finally into the big bedroom, where she put on the lights, and as the bird came directly toward the new brightness she slammed the door against it.

It could not get in here. But had it been in already? For how long had it made free of the house, shuttling through the dark rooms? And now Laurel could not get out. She was in her father's and mother's room— now Fay's room—walking up and down. It was the first time she had entered it since the morning of the funeral.

WINDOWS AND DOORS ALIKE were singing, buffeted by the storm. The bird touched, tapped, brushed itself against the walls and closed doors, never resting. Laurel thought with longing of the telephone just outside the door in the upstairs hall.

What am I in danger of here? she wondered, her heart pounding.

Even if you have kept silent for the sake of the dead, you cannot rest in your silence, as the dead rest. She listened to the wind, the rain, the blundering, frantic bird, and wanted to cry out as the nurse cried out to her, "Abuse! Abuse!"

Try to put it in the form of facts, she ordered herself. For the person who wishes to do so, it is possible to assail a helpless man; it is only necessary to be married to him. It is possible to say to the dying "Enough is enough," if the listener who overhears is his daughter with his memory to protect. The facts were a verdict, and Laurel lived with this verdict in her head, walking up and down.

It was not punishment she wanted for Fay, she wanted acknowledgment out of her—admission that she knew what she had done. And Fay, she knew now, knew beyond question, would answer, "I don't even know what you're talking about." This would be a fact. Fay had never dreamed that in that shattering moment in the hospital she had not been just as she always saw herself—in the right. Justified. Fay had only been making a little scene—that was all.

Very likely, making a scene was, for Fay, like home. Fay had brought scenes to the hospital—and here, to the house—as Mr. Dalzell's family had brought their boxes of chicken legs. Death in its reality passed her right over. Fay didn't know what she was doing—it was like Tish winking—and she never will know, Laurel thought, unless I tell her. Laurel asked herself: Have I come to be as lost a soul as the soul Fay exposed to Father, and to me? Because unlike Father, I cannot feel pity for Fay. I can't pretend it, like Mount Salus that has to live with her. I have to hold it back until she realizes what she has done.

And I can't stop realizing it, she thought. I saw Fay come out into the open. Why, it would stand up in court! Laurel thought, as she heard the bird beating against the door, and felt the house itself shake in the rainy wind. Fay betrayed herself: I'm released! she thought, shivering; one deep feeling called by its right name names others. But to be released is to tell, un-burden it.

But who could there be that she wanted to tell? Her mother. Her dead mother only. Laurel must have deeply known it from the start. She stopped at the armchair and leaned on it. She had the proof, the damnable evidence ready for her mother, and was in anguish because she could not give it to her, and so be herself consoled. The longing to tell her mother was brought about-face, and she saw the horror.

Father, beginning to lose his sight, followed Mother, but who am I at the point of following but Fay? Laurel thought. The scene she had just imagined, herself confiding the abuse to her mother, and confiding it in all tenderness, was a more devastating one than all Fay had acted out in the hospital. What would I not do, perpetrate, she wondered, for consolation?

She heard the bird drum itself against the door all its length from top to bottom. Her hands went to her hair and she backed away, backed out of the room entirely and into the little room that opened out of it.

It was the sewing room, all dark; she had to feel about for a lamp. She turned it on: her old student gooseneck lamp on a low table. By its light she saw that here was where her mother's secretary had been exiled, and her own study table, the old slipper chair; there was the brass-bound three-layer trunk; there was the sewing machine.

Even before it had been the sewing room, it had been where she slept in infancy until she was old enough to move into her own room across the hall. It was cold in here, as if there had been no fire all winter; there was only a grate, and it was empty, of course. How cold Miss Verna Longmeier's hands must have got! Laurel thought—coming here, sewing and making up tales or remembering all wrong what she saw and heard. A cold life she had lived by the day in other people's houses.

But it had been warm here, warm then. Laurel remembered her father's lean back as he sat on his haunches and spread a newspaper over the mouth of the chimney after he'd built the fire, so that the blaze caught with a sudden roar. Then he was young and could do everything.

Firelight and warmth—that was what her memory gave her. Where the secretary was now there had been her small bed, with its railed sides that could be raised as tall as she was when she stood up in bed, arms up to be lifted out. The sewing machine was still in place under the single window. When her mother—or, at her rare, appointed times, the sewing woman—sat here in her chair pedalling and whirring, Laurel sat on this floor and put together the fallen scraps of cloth into stars, flowers, birds, people, or whatever she liked to call them, lining them up, spacing them out, making them into patterns, families, on the sweet-smelling matting, with the shine of firelight, or the summer light, moving over mother and child and what they both were making.

It was quieter here. It was around the corner from the wind, and a room away from the bird and the disturbed dark. It seemed as far from the rest of the house itself as Mount Salus was from Chicago.

Laurel sat down on the slipper chair. The gooseneck lamp threw its dimmed beam on the secretary's warm brown doors. It had been made of the cherry trees on the McKelva place a long time ago; on the lid, the numerals 1817 had been set into a not quite perfect oval of different wood, something smooth and yellow as a scrap of satin. It had been built as a plantation desk but was graceful and small enough for a lady's use; Laurel's mother had had entire claim on it. On its pediment stood a lead-mold eagle spreading its wings and clasping the globe: it was about the same breadth as her mother's spread-out hand. There was no key in either keyhole of the double doors of the cabinet. But had there ever been a key? Her mother had never locked up anything that Laurel could remember. Her privacy was keyless. She had simply assumed her privacy. Now, suppose that again she would find everything was gone?

Laurel had hesitated coming to open her father's desk; she was not hesitating here—not now. She touched the doors where they met, and they swung open together. Within, the cabinet looked like a little wall out of a country post office which nobody had in years disturbed by calling for their mail. How had her mother's papers lain under merciful dust in the years past and escaped destruction? Laurel was sure of why: her father could not have borne to touch them; to Fay, they would have been only what somebody wrote— and anybody reduced to the need to write, Fay would think already beaten as a rival.

Laurel opened out the writing lid, and reaching up she drew down the letters and papers from one pigeon-hole at a time. There were twenty-six pigeonholes, but her mother had stored things according to their time and place, she discovered, not by ABC. Only the letters from her father had been all brought together, all she had received in her life, surely—there they were; the oldest envelopes had turned saffron. Laurel drew a single one out, opened the page inside long enough to see it beginning "My darling Sweetheart," and re-turned it to its place. They were postmarked from the courthouse towns her father had made sojourn in, and from Mount Salus when he addressed them to West Virginia on her visits "up home"; and under these were the letters to Miss Becky Thurston, tied in ribbons that were almost transparent, and freckled now, as the skin of her mother's hands came to be before she died. In the back of the pigeonhole where these letters came from was some solid little object, and Laurel drew it out, her fingers remembering it before she held it under her eyes. It was a two-inch bit of slatey stone, given shape by many little strokes from a penknife. It had come out of its cranny the temperature and smoothness of her skin; it fitted into her palm. "A little dish!" Laurel the child had exclaimed, thinking it something made by a child younger than she. "A boat," corrected her mother importantly. The initials C.C.M.McK. were cut running together into the base. Her father had made it himself. It had gone from his hand to her mother's; that was a river stone; they had been courting, "up home."

There was a careful record of those days preserved in a snapshot book. Laurel felt along the shelf above the pigeonholes and touched it, the square boards, the silk tassel. She pulled it down to her.

Still clinging to the first facing pages were the pair of grayed and stippled home-printed snapshots: Clinton and Becky "up home," each taken by the other standing in the same spot on a railroad track (a leafy glade), he slender as a wand, his foot on a milepost, swinging his straw hat; she with her hands full of the wildflowers they'd picked along the way.

"The most beautiful blouse I ever owned in my life —I made it. Cloth from Mother's own spinning, and dyed a deep, rich, American Beauty color with pokeberries," her mother had said with the gravity in which she spoke of "up home." "I'll never have anything to wear that to me is as satisfactory as that blouse."

How darling and vain she was when she was young! Laurel thought now. She'd made the blouse—and

developed the pictures too, for why couldn't she? And
very likely she had made the paste that held them.

Judge McKelva, who like his father had attended the
University of Virginia, had met her when he worked
one carefree year at a logging camp with quarters in
Beechy Creek, where her mother had taught school.

"Our horse was Selim. Let me hear you pronounce
his name," her mother had said to Laurel while they
sat here sewing. "I rode Selim to school. Seven miles
over Nine Mile Mountain, seven miles home. To make
the time pass quicker, I recited the whole way, from
horseback—I memorized with no great effort, dear,"
she'd replied to the child's protest. "Papa hadn't had
an entirely easy time of it, getting books at all up
home."

Laurel had been taken "up home" since a summer
before she remembered. The house was built on top
of what might as well have been already the highest
roof in the world. There were rocking chairs outside
it on the sweet, roofless green grass. From a rocking
chair could be seen the river where it rounded the
foot of the mountain. It was only when you wound
your way down the mountain nearly to the bottom
that you began to hear the river. It sounded like a
roomful of mesmerized schoolchildren reciting to
their teacher. This point of the river was called Queen's
Shoals.

Both Becky's father and her mother had been Vir-
ginians. The mother's family (fathered by a line of

preachers and teachers) had packed up and gone across the border around the time of the Secession. Becky's own father had been a lawyer, too. But the mountain had stood five times as high as the courthouse roof, straight up behind it, and the river went rushing in front of it like a road. It was its only road.

They must have had names. Laurel never remembered hearing them said. They were just "the mountain," "the river," "the courthouse," parts of "up home."

In the early morning, from the next mountain, from one stillness to another, travelled the sound of a blow, then behind it its echo, then another blow, then the echo, then a shouting and the shouting falling back on itself. On it went.

"Mother, what are they doing?" Laurel asked.

"It's just an old man chopping wood," said "the boys."

"He's praying," said her mother.

"An old hermit that is," said Grandma. "Without a soul in the world."

"The boys"—there were six—saddled the pony for their sister; then they rode off with her. They lay on blankets and saddles under the apple tree and played the banjo for her. They told her so many stories she cried, all about people only she knew and they knew; had she not cried she would have never been able to stop laughing. Of her youngest brother, who sang "Billy Boy" and banged comically on the strings, she said, "Very well for Sam. He went out and cried on the ground when I married."

In sight of the door there was an iron bell mounted on a post. If anything were ever to happen, Grandma only needed to ring this bell.

The first time Laurel could remember arriving in West Virginia instead of just finding herself there, her mother and she had got down from the train in early morning and stood, after it had gone, by themselves on a steep rock, all of the world that they could see in the mist being their rock and its own iron bell on a post with its rope hanging down. Her mother gave the rope a pull and at its sound, almost at the moment of it, large and close to them appeared a gray boat with two of the boys at the oars. At their very feet had been the river. The boat came breasting out of the mist, and in they stepped. All new things in life were meant to come like that.

Bird dogs went streaking the upslanted pasture through the sweet long grass that swept them as high as their noses. While it was still day on top of the mountain, the light still warm on the cheek, the valley was dyed blue under them. While one of "the boys" was coming up, his white shirt would shine for a long time almost without moving in her sight, like Venus in the sky of Mount Salus, while grandmother, mother, and little girl sat, outlasting the light, waiting for him to climb home.

Wings beat again. Flying in from over the mountain, over the roof and a child's head, high up in blue air, pigeons had formed a cluster and twinkled as one body. Like a great sheet of cloth whipping in a wind of its own making, they were about her ears. They came down to her feet and walked on the mountain. Laurel was afraid of them, but she had been provided with biscuits from the table to feed them with. They walked about, opalescent and solid, on worm-pink feet, each bird marked a little differently from the rest and each with a voice soft as a person's.

Laurel had stood panic-stricken, holding a biscuit in a frozen gesture of appeal.

"They're just Grandma's pigeons."

Her grandmother smoothed Laurel's already too straight hair and pushed it behind her ears. "They're just hungry."

But Laurel had kept the pigeons under eye in their pigeon house and had already seen a pair of them sticking their beaks down each other's throats, gagging each other, eating out of each other's craws, swallowing down all over again what had been swallowed before: they were taking turns. The first time, she hoped they might never do it again, but they did it again next day while the other pigeons copied them. They convinced her that they could not escape each other and could not themselves be escaped from. So when the pigeons flew down, she tried to position herself behind her grandmother's skirt, which was long and black, but her grandmother said again, "They're just hungry, like we are."

No more than Laurel had known that rivers ran clear and sang over rocks might her mother have known that *her* mother's pigeons were waiting to pluck each other's tongues out. "Up home," just as Laurel was in Mount Salus, her mother was too happy to know what went on in the outside world. Besides, when her mother looked closely, it was not in order to see pigeons but to verify something—the truth or a mistake; hers or another's. Laurel was ashamed to tell anybody else before she told her mother; as a result the pigeons were considered Laurel's pets.

"Come on!" cried "the boys" to Grandma. "*Let* the little beggar feed her pigeons!"

Parents and children take turns back and forth, changing places, protecting and protesting each other: so it seemed to the child.

Sometimes the top of the mountain was higher than the flying birds. Sometimes even clouds lay down the hill, hiding the treetops farther down. The highest house, the deepest well, the tuning of the strings; sleep in the clouds; Queen's Shoals; the fastest conversations on earth—no wonder her mother needed nothing else! Eventually her father would come for them—he would be called "Mr. McKelva"; and they would go home on the train. They had taken a trunk with them —*this* trunk, with all the dresses made in this room: they might have stayed always. Her father had not appeared to realize it. They came back to Mount Salus. "Where do they get the *mount*?" her mother said scornfully. "There's no 'mount' here."

Grandma had died unexpectedly; she was alone. From the top of the stairs Laurel had heard her mother crying uncontrollably: the first time she had ever heard anyone cry uncontrollably except herself.

"I wasn't there! I wasn't *there!*"

"You are not to blame yourself, Becky, do you hear me?"

"You can't make me lie to myself, Clinton!"

They raised their voices, cried out back and forth, as if grief could be fabricated into an argument to comfort itself with. When, some time later, Laurel asked about the bell, her mother replied calmly that how good a bell was depended on the distance away your children had gone.

Laurel's own mother, after her sight was gone, lay in bed in the big room reciting to herself sometimes as she had done on horseback at sixteen to make the long ride over the mountain go faster. She did not like being read to, *she* preferred to do the reading, she said now. " 'If the salt have lost his savor, wherewith shall it be salted?' " she had asked, the most reckless expression on her wasted face. She knew Dr. Courtland's step, and greeted him with " 'Man, proud man! Dress't in a little brief authority!' "

"Don't let them tie me down," her mother had

whispered on the evening before the last of the operations. "If they try to hold me, I'll die."

Judge McKelva had let this pass, but Laurel had said, "I know—you're quoting the words of your own father."

She had nodded at them fervently.

When she was fifteen years old, Becky had gone with her father, who was suffering pain, on a raft propelled by a neighbor, down the river at night when it was filled with ice, to reach a railroad, to wave a lantern at a snowy train that would stop and take them on, to reach a hospital.

("How could you make a fire on a raft?" asked Laurel, here on this matting. "How could a fire burn on water?" "We had to have a fire," said her mother, sewing on her fingers. "We *made* it burn.")

In the city of Baltimore, when at last they reached the hospital, the little girl entrusted the doctors with what he had told her: "Papa said, 'If you let them tie me down, I'll die.' " He could not by then have told the doctors for himself; he was in delirium. It turned out that he had suffered a ruptured appendix.

Two doctors came out of the operating room, to where Becky stood waiting in the hall. One said, "You'd better get in touch with whoever you know in Baltimore, little girl." "But I don't know anybody in Baltimore, sir." "Not know anybody in *Baltimore?*"

This incredulity on the part of the hospital was the

memory that had stayed sharpest in Becky's mind, although afterwards she had ridden home in the baggage car of the train, guided herself back to her mother and the houseful of little boys, bearing the news and bringing the coffin, both together.

Neither of us saved our fathers, Laurel thought. But Becky was the brave one. I stood in the hall, too, but I did not any longer believe that anyone could be saved, anyone at all. Not from others.

The house shook suddenly and seemed to go on shaking after a long roll of thunder.

"Up home, we loved a good storm coming, we'd fly outdoors and run up and down to meet it," her mother used to say. "We children would run as fast as we could go along the top of that mountain when the wind was blowing, holding our arms wide open. The wilder it blew the better we liked it." During the very bursting of a tornado which carried away half of Mount Salus, she said, "*We* never were afraid of a little wind. Up home, we'd welcome a good storm."

"You don't know anybody in Baltimore?" they had asked Becky.

But Becky had known herself.

There had been so much confidence when first her vision had troubled her. Laurel remembered how her mother, early in the morning of her first eye operation (and after an injection supposed to make her

sleepy), was affected with the gayest high spirits and
anticipation, and had asked for her dressing case, and
before the inadequate mirror had powdered and
dabbed rouge on her face and put on a touch of lipstick and even sprayed about with her scent, as though
she had been going to an evening party with her husband. She had stretched out her hand in exhilaration
to the orderly who came to wheel her out, as if after
Nate Courtland had removed that little cataract in the
Mount Salus Hospital, she would wake up and be in
West Virginia.

When someone lies sick and troubled for five years
and is beloved, unforeseen partisanship can spring up
among the well. During her mother's long trial in
bed, Laurel, young and recently widowed, had somehow turned for a while against her father: he seemed
so particularly helpless to do anything for his wife.
He was not passionately enough grieved at the changes
in her! He seemed to give the changes his same, kind
recognition—to accept them because they had to be
only of the time being, even to love them, even to
laugh sometimes at their absurdity. "Why do you
persist in letting them hurt me?" her mother would
ask him. Laurel battled against them both, each for
the other's sake. She loyally reproached her mother
for yielding to the storms that began coming to her
out of her darkness of vision. Her mother had only
to recollect herself! As for her father, he apparently
needed guidance in order to see the tragic.

What burdens we lay on the dying, Laurel thought, as she listened now to the accelerated rain on the roof: seeking to prove some little thing that we can keep to comfort us when they can no longer feel—something as incapable of being kept as of being proved: the lastingness of memory, vigilance against harm, self-reliance, good hope, trust in one another.

Her father in his domestic gentleness had a horror of any sort of private clash, of divergence from the affectionate and the real and the explainable and the recognizable. He was a man of great delicacy; what he had not been born with he had learned in reaching toward his wife. He grimaced with delicacy. What he could not control was his belief that all his wife's troubles would turn out all right because there was nothing he would not have given her. When he reached a loss he simply put on his hat and went speechless out of the house to his office and worked for an hour or so getting up a brief for somebody.

"Laurel, open my desk drawer and hand me my old McGuffey's Fifth Reader," her mother would some-times say while she sat there alone with her. It had become a book of reference. Laurel's hand, now, drew open the drawer of the desk, and there lay McGuffey. She took it out and let it fall open. "The Cataract of Lodore." She could imagine every word on the page being recited in her mother's voice—not the young mother who had learned it on her mountain, but the mother blind, in this house, in the next room, in her bed.

> ... *"Rising and leaping—*
> *Sinking and creeping,*
> *Swelling and sweeping—*
> *Showering and springing,*
> *Flying and flinging,*
> *Writhing and ringing ...*
>
> *Turning and twisting,*
> *Around and around*
> *With endless rebound;*
> *Smiting and fighting,*
> *A sight to delight in;*
> *Confounding, astounding—"*

Whatever she recited she put the same deep feeling into. With her voice she was saying that the more she could call back of "The Cataract of Lodore," the better she could defend her case in some trial that seemed to be going on against her life.

> *"And glittering and frittering,*
> *And gathering and feathering,*
> *And whitening and brightening,*
> *And quivering and shivering,*
> *And hurrying and skurrying,*
> *And thundering and floundering ..."*

Then when he'd come home, her father would stand helpless in bewilderment by his wife's bed. Spent, she had whispered, "Why did I marry a coward?"—then had taken his hand to help him bear it.

Later still, she began to say—and her voice never weakened, never harshened, it was her spirit speaking in the wrong words—"All you do is hurt me. I wish I might know what it is I've done. Why is it necessary to punish me like this and not tell me why?" And still she held fast to their hands, to Laurel's too. Her cry was not complaint; it was anger at wanting to know and being denied knowledge; it was love's deep anger.

"Becky, it's going to be all right," Judge McKelva whispered to her.

"I've heard that before."

One day her mother had from her torments gasped out the words, "I need spiritual guidance!" She, who had dared any McKelva missionary to speak his piece to her, sent out through Laurel an invitation to the Presbyterian preacher to call upon her soon. Dr. Bolt was young then, and appealing to women—Miss Tennyson Bullock used to say so; but his visit upstairs here had not been well taken. He had begun by reading her a psalm, which she recited along with him. Her tongue was faster than his. When he was left behind on everything he tried, she told him, "I'd like better than anything you can tell me just to see the mountain one more time." When he wondered if God intended her to, she put in a barb: "And on that mountain, young man, there's a white strawberry that grows completely in the wild, if you know where to look for it. I think it very likely grows in only one spot in the world. I could tell you this minute where to go, but I doubt if you'd see them growing after you got there. Deep in the woods, you'd miss them. You could find them by mistake, and you could line your hat with leaves and try to walk off with a hatful: that would be how little you knew about those berries. Once you've let them so much as touch each other, you've already done enough to finish 'em." She fixed him with her nearly sightless eyes. "Nothing you ever ate in your life was anything like as delicate, as fragrant, as those wild white strawberries. You had to know enough to go where they are and stand and eat them on the spot, that's all."

"I'll take you back to your mountains, Becky," her father had said into the despairing face after Dr. Bolt had tiptoed away. Laurel was certain it was the first worthless promise that had ever lain between them. And the house on the mountain had by that time, anyway, burned. Laurel had been in camp the summer it happened; but her mother had been "up home." She had run back into the flames and rescued her dead father's set of Dickens at the risk of her life, and brought the books down to Mount Salus and made room for them in the library bookcase, and there they stood now. But before she died it had slipped her mind that the house had ever burned down at all.

"I'll carry you there, Becky."

"Lucifer!" she cried. "*Liar!*"

That was when he started, of course, being what he scowlingly called an optimist; he might have dredged the word up out of his childhood. He loved his wife. Whatever she did that she couldn't help doing was all right. Whatever she was driven to say was all right. But it was *not* all right! Her trouble was that very desperation. And no one had the power to cause that except the one she desperately loved, who refused to consider that she was desperate. It was betrayal on betrayal.

In her need tonight Laurel would have been willing to wish her mother and father dragged back to any torment of living because that torment was something they had known together, through each other. She wanted them with her to share her grief as she had been the sharer of theirs. She sat and thought of only one thing, of her mother holding and holding onto their hands, her own and her father's holding onto her mother's, long after there was nothing more to be said.

Laurel could remember, too, her mother holding her own hands before her eyes, very close, so that she seemed to be seeing them, the empty, working fingers.

"Poor hands in winter, when she came back from

the well—bleeding from the ice, from the *ice!*" her mother cried.

"Who, Mother?" Laurel asked.

"*My* mother!" she cried accusingly.

After a stroke had crippled her further, she had come to believe—without being able to see her room, see a face, to verify anything by seeing—that she had been taken somewhere that was neither home nor "up home," that she was left among strangers, for whom even anger meant nothing, on whom it would only be wasted. She had died without speaking a word, keeping everything to herself, in exile and humiliation.

To Laurel while she still knew her, she had made a last remark: "You could have saved your mother's life. But you stood by and wouldn't intervene. I despair for you."

Baltimore was as far a place as you could go with those you loved, and it was where they left you.

Then Laurel's father, when he was approaching seventy, had married Fay. Both times he chose, he had suffered; she had seen him contain it. He died worn out with both wives—almost as if up to the last he had still had both of them.

As he lay without moving in the hospital he had concentrated utterly on time passing, indeed he had. But which way had it been going for him? When he could no longer get up and encourage it, push it forward, had it turned on him, started moving back the other way?

Fay had once at least called Becky "my rival." Laurel thought: But the rivalry doesn't lie where Fay thinks. It's not between the living and the dead, between the old wife and the new; it's between too much love and too little. There is no rivalry as bitter; Laurel had seen its work.

Later and later into the night, with the buffeting kept at its distance, though it never let up, Laurel sat under the lamp among the papers. She held in her hands her mother's yellowed notebooks—correspondence records, address books—Virginia aunts and cousins long dead, West Virginia nieces and nephews now married and moved where Laurel no longer quite kept up with them. The brothers had moved down the mountain into town, into the city, and the banjo player who had known so many verses to "Where Have You Been, Billy Boy?" had turned into a bank official. Only the youngest had been able to come to Mount Salus to his sister's funeral. He who had been the Evening Star climbed on two canes to her grave and said to Judge McKelva, as they stood together, "She's a long way from West Virginia."

A familiar black-covered "composition book" came off the shelf and lay open on Laurel's lap to "My Best Bread," written out twenty or thirty years ago in her mother's strict, pointed hand, giving everything but the steps of procedure. ("A cook is not exactly a fool.") Underneath it had lain something older, a class note-book. Becky had sent herself to teacher's college, wearing the deep-dyed blouse. It was her *keeping* her diagrams of *Paradise Lost* and Milton's Universe that was so like her, pigeonholing them here as though she'd be likely to find them useful again. Laurel gazed down at the careful figuring of the modest household accounts, drifted along the lined pages (this was an old Mount Salus Bank book) to where they eased into garden diaries and the plots of her rose beds, her perennial borders. "I have just come in. Clinton is still toiling. I see him now from my kitchen window, struggling with the Mermaid rose." "That fool fig tree is already putting out leaves. Will it never learn?"

The last pigeonhole held letters her mother had saved from her own mother, from "up home."

She slipped them from their thin envelopes and read them now for herself. Widowed, her health failing, lonely and sometimes bedridden, Grandma wrote these letters to her young, venturesome, defiant, happily married daughter as to an exile, without ever allowing herself to put it into so many words. Laurel could hardly believe the bravery and serenity she had put into these short letters, in the quickened pencil to catch the pocket of one of "the boys" before he rode off again, dependent—Grandma then, as much as Laurel now— upon his remembering to mail them from "the court-house." She read on and met her own name on a page.

"I will try to send Laurel a cup of sugar for her birthday. Though if I can find a way to do it, I would like to send her one of my pigeons. It would eat from her hand, if she would let it."

A flood of feeling descended on Laurel. She let the papers slide from her hand and the books from her knees, and put her head down on the open lid of the desk and wept in grief for love and for the dead. She lay there with all that was adamant in her yielding to this night, yielding at last. Now all she had found had found her. The deepest spring in her heart had uncovered itself, and it began to flow again.

If Phil could have lived—

But Phil was lost. Nothing of their life together remained except in her own memory; love was sealed away into its perfection and had remained there.

If Phil had lived—

She had gone on living with the old perfection undisturbed and undisturbing. Now, by her own hands, the past had been raised up, and *he* looked at her, Phil himself—here waiting, all the time, Lazarus. He looked at her out of eyes wild with the craving for his unlived life, with mouth open like a funnel's.

What would have been their end, then? Suppose their marriage had ended like her father and mother's? Or like her mother's father and mother's? Like—

"Laurel! Laurel! Laurel!" Phil's voice cried.

She wept for what happened to life.

"I wanted it!" Phil cried. His voice rose with the wind in the night and went around the house and around the house. It became a roar. "I wanted it!"

Four

SHE HAD SLEPT in the chair, like a passenger who had come on an emergency journey in a train. But she had rested deeply.

She had dreamed that she *was* a passenger, and riding with Phil. They had ridden together over a long bridge.

Awake, she recognized it: it was a dream of something that had really happened. When she and Phil were coming down from Chicago to Mount Salus to be married in the Presbyterian Church, they came on the train. Laurel, when she travelled back and forth between Mount Salus and Chicago, had always taken the sleeper—the same crack train she had just ridden from New Orleans. She and Phil followed the route on the day train, and she saw it for the first time.

When they were climbing the long approach to a bridge after leaving Cairo, rising slowly higher until they rode above the tops of bare trees, she looked down and saw the pale light widening and the river bottoms opening out, and then the water appearing, reflecting the low, early sun. There were two rivers. Here was where they came together. This was the confluence of the waters, the Ohio and the Mississippi.

They were looking down from a great elevation and all they saw was at the point of coming together, the bare trees marching in from the horizon, the rivers moving into one, and as he touched her arm she looked up with him and saw the long, ragged, pencil-faint line of birds within the crystal of the zenith, flying in a V of their own, following the same course down. All they could see was sky, water, birds, light, and confluence. It was the whole morning world.

And they themselves were a part of the confluence. Their own joint act of faith had brought them here at the very moment and matched its occurrence, and proceeded as it proceeded. Direction itself was made beautiful, momentous. They were riding as one with it, right up front. It's our turn! she'd thought exultantly. And we're going to live forever.

Left bodiless and graveless of a death made of water and fire in a year long gone, Phil could still tell her of her life. For her life, any life, she had to believe, was nothing but the continuity of its love.

She believed it just as she believed that the confluence of the waters was still happening at Cairo. It would be there the same as it ever was when she went flying over it today on her way back—out of sight, for her, this time, thousands of feet below, but with nothing in between except thin air.

Philip Hand was an Ohio country boy. He had a country boy's soft-spokenness and selfless energy and long-range plans. He had put himself through architectural school—Georgia Tech, because it was cheaper and warmer there—in her country; then had met her when she came north to study in his, at the Art Institute in Chicago. From far back, generations, they must have had common memories. (Ohio was across the river from West Virginia; the Ohio was his river.)

But there was nothing like a kinship between them, as they learned. In life and in work and in affection they were each shy, each bold, just where the other was not. She grew up in the kind of shyness that takes its refuge in giving refuge. Until she knew Phil, she thought of love as shelter; her arms went out as a naïve offer of safety. He had showed her that this need not be so. Protection, like self-protection, fell away from her like all one garment, some anachronism foolishly saved from childhood.

Philip had large, good hands, and extraordinary thumbs—double-jointed where they left the palms, nearly at right angles; their long, blunt tips curved strongly back. When she watched his right hand go about its work, it looked to her like the Hand of his name.

She had a certain gift of her own. He taught her, through his example, how to use it. She learned how to work by working beside him. He taught her to draw, to work toward and into her pattern, not to sketch peripheries.

Designing houses was not enough for his energy. He fitted up a workshop in their South Side apartment, taking up half the kitchen. "I get a moral satisfaction out of putting things together," he said. "I like to see a thing finished." He made simple objects of immediate use, taking unlimited pains. What he was, was a perfectionist.

But he was not an optimist—she knew that. Phil had learned everything he could manage to learn, and done as much as he had time for, to design houses to stand, to last, to be lived in; but he had known they could equally well, with the same devotion and tireless effort, be built of cards.

When the country went to war, Philip said, "Not the Army, not the Engineers. I've heard what happens to architects. They get put in Camouflage. This war's got to move too fast to stop for junk like camouflage." He went into the Navy and ended up as a communications officer on board a mine sweeper in the Pacific.

Taking the train, Laurel's father made his first trip to Chicago in years to see Phil on his last leave. (Her mother was unable to travel anywhere except "up home.")

"How close have those *kamikaze* come to you so far, son?" the Judge wanted to know.

"About close enough to shake hands with," Phil said.

A month later, they came closer still.

As far as Laurel had ever known, there had not happened a single blunder in their short life together. But the guilt of outliving those you love is justly to be borne, she thought. Outliving is something we do to them. The fantasies of dying could be no stranger than the fantasies of living. Surviving is perhaps the strangest fantasy of them all.

The house was bright and still, like a ship that has tossed all night and come to harbor. She had not forgotten what waited for her today. Turning off the panicky lights of last night as she went, she walked through the big bedroom and opened the door into the hall.

She saw the bird at once, high up in a fold of the curtain at the stair window; it was still, too, and narrowed, wings to its body.

As the top step of the stairs creaked under her foot, the bird quivered its wings rapidly without altering its position. She sped down the stairs and closed herself into the kitchen while she planned and breakfasted. She'd got upstairs again and dressed and come out again, still to find the bird had not moved from its position.

Loudly, like a clumsy, slow echo of the wingbeating, a pounding began on the front porch. It was no effort any longer to remember anybody: Laurel knew there was only one man in Mount Salus who knocked like that, the perennial jack-leg carpenter who appeared in spring to put in new window cords, sharpen the lawn mower, plane off the back screen door from its wintertime sag. He still acted, no doubt, for widows and maiden ladies and for wives whose husbands were helpless around the house.

"Well, this time it's your dad. Old Miss been gone a dozen year. I miss her ever' time I pass the old place," said Mr. Cheek. "Her and her ideas."

Was this some last, misguided call of condolence? "What is it, Mr. Cheek?" she asked.

"Locks holding?" he asked. "Ready for me to string your window cords? Change your furniture around?" He was the same. He mounted the steps and came right across the porch at a march, with his knees bent and turned out, and the tools knocking together inside his sack.

Her mother had deplored his familiar ways and blundering hammer, had called him on his cheating, and would have sent him packing for good the first time she heard him refer to her as "Old Miss." Now he was moving into what he must suppose was a clear field. "Roof do any leaking last night?"

"No. A bird came down the chimney, that's all," said Laurel. "If you'd like to be useful, I'll let you get it out for me."

"Bird in the house?" he asked. "Sign o' bad luck, ain't it?" He still walked up the stairs with a strut and followed too close. "I reckon I'm elected."

The bird had not moved from its position. Heavy-looking, laden with soot, it was still pressed into the same curtain fold.

"I spot him!" Mr. Cheek shouted. He stamped his

foot, then clogged with both feet like a clown, and the bird dropped from the curtain into flight and, barely missing the wall, angled into Laurel's room—her bedroom door had come open. Mr. Cheek with a shout slammed the door on it.

"Mr. Cheek!"

"Well, I got him out of your hall."

Laurel's door opened again, of itself, with a slowness that testified there was nothing behind it but the morning breeze.

"I'm not prepared for a joke this morning," Laurel said. "I want that bird out of my room!"

Mr. Cheek marched on into her bedroom. His eye slid to the muslin curtains, wet, with the starch rained out of them—she realized that her window had been open all night—where the shineless bird was frantically striking itself; but she could see he was only sizing up the frayed window cords.

"It'll get in every room in the house if you let it," Laurel said, controlling herself from putting her hands over her hair.

"It ain't trying to get in. Trying to get out," said Mr. Cheek, and crowed at her. He marched around the room, glancing into Laurel's suitcase, opened out on the bed—there was nothing for him to see, only her sketchbook that she'd never taken out—and inspected the dressing table and himself in its mirror, while the bird tried itself from curtain to curtain and spurted out of the room ahead of him. It had left the dust of itself all over everything, the way a moth does.

"Where's Young Miss?" asked Mr. Cheek, and opened the big bedroom door. The bird flew in like an arrow.

"Mr. Cheek!"

"That's about my favorite room in the house," he said. He gave Laurel a black grin; his front teeth had gone.

"Mr. Cheek, I thought I told you—I wasn't ready for a joke. You've simply come and made things worse than you found them. Exactly like you used to do!" Laurel said.

"Well, I won't charge you nothing," he said, clattering down the stairs behind her. "I don't see nothing wrong with you," he added. "Why didn't you ever go 'head and marry you another somebody?"

She walked to the door and waited for him to leave. He laughed good-naturedly. "Yep, I'm all that's left of my folks too," he said. "Maybe me and you ought to get together."

"Mr. Cheek, I'd be very glad if you'd depart."

"If you don't sound like Old Miss!" he said admiringly. "No hard feelings," he called, skipping into his escape down the steps. "You even got her voice."

Missouri had arrived; she came out with her broom to the front porch. "What happen?"

"A chimney swift! A chimney swift got out of the fireplace into the house and flew everywhere," Laurel said. "It's still loose upstairs."

"It's because we get it all too clean, brag too soon," said Missouri. "You didn't ask that Mr. Cheeks? He just waltz through the house enjoying the scenery, what I bet."

"He was a failure. We'll shoo it out between us."

"That's what it look like. It's just me and you."

Missouri, when she appeared again, was stuffed back into her raincoat and hat and buckled in tight. She walked slowly up the stairs holding the kitchen broom, bristles up.

"Do you see it?" Laurel asked. She saw the mark on the stairway curtain where the bird had tried to stay asleep. She heard it somewhere, ticking.

"He on the telephone."

"Oh, don't hit—"

"How'm I gonna git him, then? Look," said Missouri. "He ain't got no business in your room."

"Just move behind it. Birds fly toward light—I'm sure I've been told. Here—I'm holding the front door wide open for it." Missouri could be heard dropping the broom. "It's got a perfectly clear way out now," Laurel called. "Why won't it just fly free of its own accord?"

"They just ain't got no sense like we have."

Laurel propped the screen door open and ran upstairs with two straw wastebaskets. "I'll *make* it go free."

Then her heart sank. The bird was down on the floor, under the telephone table. It looked small and unbearably flat to the ground, like a child's shoe without a foot inside it.

"Missouri, I've always been scared one would touch me," Laurel told her. "I'll tell *you* that." It looked eyeless, unborn, so still was it holding.

"They vermin," said Missouri.

Laurel dropped the first basket over the bird, then cupped the two baskets together to enclose it; the whole operation was soundless and over in an instant.

"What if I've hurt it?"

"Cat'll git him, that's all."

Laurel ran down the stairs and out of the house and down the front steps, not a step of the way without the knowledge of what she carried, vibrating through the ribs of the baskets, the beat of its wings or of its heart, its blind struggle against rescue.

On the front sidewalk, she got ready.

"What you doing?" called old Mrs. Pease through her window curtains. "Thought you were due to be gone!"

"I am, just about!" called Laurel, and opened the baskets.

Something struck her face—not feathers; it was a blow of wind. The bird was away. In the air it was nothing but a pair of wings—she saw no body any more, no tail, just a tilting crescent being drawn back into the sky.

"All birds got to fly, even them no-count dirty ones,"

said Missouri from the porch. "Now I got all that wrenching out to do over."

For the next hour, Laurel stood in the driveway burning her father's letters to her mother, and Grandma's letters, and the saved little books and papers in the rusty wire basket where pecan leaves used to get burned—"too acid for my roses." She burned Milton's Universe. She saw the words "this morning?" with the uncompromising hook of her mother's question mark, on a little round scrap of paper that was slowly growing smaller in the smoke. She had a child's desire to reach for it, like a coin left lying in the street for any passer-by to find and legitimately keep—by then it was consumed. All Laurel would have wanted with her mother's "this morning?" would have been to make it over, give her a new one in its place. She stood humbly holding the blackened rake. She thought of her father.

The smoke dimmed the dogwood tree like a veil over a face that might have shone with too naked a candor. Miss Adele Courtland was hurrying under it now, at a fast teacher's walk, to tell Laurel goodbye before time for school. She looked at what Laurel was doing and her face withheld judgment.

"There's one thing—I'd like you to keep it," said Laurel. She reached in her apron pocket for it.

"Polly. You mustn't give this up. You must know I can't allow you—no, indeed, you must cling to this." She pressed the little soapstone boat back into Laurel's hand quickly, told her goodbye, and fled away to her school.

Laurel had presumed. And no one would ever succeed in comforting Miss Adele Courtland, anyway: she would only comfort the comforter.

Upstairs, Laurel folded her slacks and the wrinkled silk dress of last night into her case, dropped in the other few things she'd brought, and closed it. Then she bathed and dressed again in the Sibyl Connolly suit she'd flown down in. She was careful with her lipstick, and pinned her hair up for Chicago. She stepped back into her city heels, and started on a last circuit through the house. All the windows, which Missouri had patiently stripped so as to wash the curtains over again, let in the full volume of spring light. There was nothing she was leaving in the whole shining and quiet house now to show for her mother's life and her mother's happiness and suffering, and nothing to show for Fay's harm; her father's turning between them, holding onto them both, then letting them go, was without any sign.

From the stair window she could see that the crab-apple tree had rushed into green, all but one sleeve that was still flowery.

The last of the funeral flowers had been carried out of the parlor—the tulips, that had stayed beautiful until the last petal fell. Over the white-painted mantel, where cranes in their circle of moon, the beggar with his lantern, the poet at his waterfall hung in their positions around the clock, the hour showed thirty minutes before noon.

She was prepared for the bridesmaids.

And then, from the back of the house, she heard a sound—like an empty wooden spool dropped down through a cupboard and rolling away. She walked into the kitchen, where through the open door she could see Missouri just beginning to hang out her curtains. The room was still odorous of hot soapsuds.

The same wooden kitchen table of her childhood, strong as the base of an old square piano, stood bare in the middle of the wooden floor. There were two cupboards, and only the new one, made of metal, was in daily use. The original wooden one Laurel had somehow passed over in her work, as forgetfully as she'd left her own window open to the rain. She advanced on it, tugged at the wooden doors until they gave. She opened them and got the earnest smell of mouse.

In the dark interior she made out the fruitcake pans, the sack of ice-cream salt, the waffle irons, the punch bowl hung with its cups and glinting with the oily rainbows of neglect. Underneath all those useless things, shoved back as far as it would go but still on the point of pushing itself out of the cupboard, something was waiting for her to find; and she was still here, to find it.

Kneeling, moving the objects rapidly out of her way, Laurel reached with both hands and drew it out into the light of the curtainless day and looked at it. It was exactly what she thought it was. In that same moment, she felt, more sharply than she could hear them where she was, footsteps that tracked through the parlor, the library, the hall, the dining room, up the stairs and through the bedrooms, down the stairs, in the same path Laurel had taken, and at last came to the kitchen door and stopped.

"You mean to tell me you're still here?" Fay said.

Laurel said, "What have you done to my mother's breadboard?"

"*Breadboard?*"

Laurel rose and carried it to the middle of the room and set it on the table. She pointed. "Look. Look where the surface is splintered—look at those gouges. You might have gone at it with an icepick."

"Is that a crime?"

"All scored and grimy! Or you tried driving nails in it."

"I didn't do anything but crack last year's walnuts on it. With the hammer."

"And cigarette burns—"

"Who wants an everlasting breadboard? It's the last thing on earth anybody needs!"

"And there—along the edge!" With a finger that was trembling now, Laurel drew along it.

"Most likely a house as old as this has got a few enterprising rats in it," Fay said.

"Gnawed and blackened and the dust ground into it —Mother kept it satin-smooth, and clean as a dish!"

"It's just an old board, isn't it?" cried Fay.

"She made the best bread in Mount Salus!"

"All right! Who cares? She's not making it now."

"You desecrated this house."

"I don't know what that word means, and glad I don't. But I'll have you remember it's my house now, and I can do what I want to with it," Fay said. "With everything in it. And that goes for that breadboard too."

And all Laurel had felt and known in the night, all she'd remembered, and as much as she could understand this morning—in the week at home, the month, in her life—could not tell her now how to stand and face the person whose own life had not taught her how to feel. Laurel didn't know even how to tell her goodbye.

"Fay, my mother knew you'd get in her house. She never needed to be told," said Laurel. "She predicted you."

"Predict? You *predict* the *weather*," said Fay.

You *are* the weather, thought Laurel. And the weather to come: there'll be many a one more like you, in this life.

"She predicted you."

Experience did, finally, get set into its right order, which is not always the order of other people's time. Her mother had suffered in life every symptom of having been betrayed, and it was not until she had died, and the protests of memory came due, that Fay had ever tripped in from Madrid, Texas. It was not until that later moment, perhaps, that her father himself had ever dreamed of a Fay. For Fay was Becky's own dread. What Becky had felt, and had been afraid of, might have existed right here in the house all the time, for her. Past and future might have changed places, in some convulsion of the mind, but that could do nothing to impugn the truth of the heart. Fay could have walked in early as well as late, she could have come at any time at all. She was coming.

"But your mother, she died a crazy!" Fay cried.

"Fay, that is not true. And nobody ever dared to say such a thing."

"In Mount Salus? I heard it in Mount Salus, right in this house. Mr. Cheek put me wise. He told me how he went in my room one day while she was alive and she threw something at him."

"Stop," said Laurel.

"It was the little bell off her table. She told him she deliberately aimed at his knee, because she didn't have a wish to hurt any living creature. She was a crazy and you'll be a crazy too, if you don't watch out."

"My mother never did hurt any living creature."

"Crazies never did scare me. You can't scare me into running away, either. You're the one that's got to do the running," Fay said.

"Scaring people into things. Scaring people out of things. You haven't learned any better yet, Fay?" Trembling, Laurel kept on. "What were you trying to scare Father into—when you struck him?"

"I was trying to scare him into living!" Fay cried.

"You what? You *what?*"

"I wanted him to get up out of there, and start him paying a little attention to *me,* for a change."

"He was dying," said Laurel. "He was paying full attention to that."

"I tried to make him quit his old-man foolishness. I was going to make him live if I had to drag him! And I take good credit for what I did!" cried Fay. "It's more than anybody else was doing."

"You hurt him."

"I was being a wife to him!" cried Fay. "Have you clean forgotten by this time what being a wife is?"

"I haven't forgotten," Laurel said. "Do you want to know why this breadboard right here is such a beautiful piece of work? I can tell you. It's because my husband made it."

"*Made* it? What for?"

"Do you know what a labor of love is? My husband made it for my mother, so she'd have a good one. Phil had the gift—the gift of his hands. And he planed—fitted—glued—clamped—it's made on the true, look and see, it's still as straight as his T-square. Tongued and grooved—tight-fitted, every edge—"

"I couldn't care less," said Fay.

"I watched him make it. He's the one in the family who could make things. We were a family of comparatively helpless people—that's what so bound us, bound us together. My mother blessed him when she saw this. She said it was sound and beautiful and exactly suited her long-felt needs, and she welcomed it into her kitchen."

"It's mine now," said Fay.

"But I'm the one that's going to take care of it," said Laurel.

"You mean you're asking me to give it to you?"

"I'm going to take it back to Chicago with me."

"What makes you think I'll let you? What's made you so brazen all at once?"

"Finding the breadboard!" Laurel cried. She placed both hands down on it and gave it the weight of her body.

"Fine Miss Laurel!" said Fay. "If they all could see you now! You mean you'd carry it out of the house the way it is? It's dirty as sin."

"A coat of grime is something I can get rid of."

"If all you want to do is rub the skin off your bones."

"The scars it's got are a different matter. But I'd work."

"And do what with it when you got through?" Fay said mockingly.

"Have my try at making bread. Only last night, by the grace of God, I had my mother's recipe, written in her own hand, right before my eyes."

"It all tastes alike, don't it?"

"You never tasted my mother's. I could turn out a good loaf too—I'd work at it."

"And then who'd eat it with you?" said Fay.

"Phil loved bread. He loved good bread. To break a loaf and eat it warm, just out of the oven," Laurel said. Ghosts. And in irony she saw herself, pursuing her own way through the house as single-mindedly as Fay had pursued hers through the ceremony of the day of the funeral. But of course they had had to come together—it was useless to suppose they wouldn't meet, here at the end of it. Laurel was not late, not yet, in leaving, but Fay had come early, and in time. For there is hate as well as love, she supposed, in the coming together and continuing of our lives. She thought of Phil and the *kamikaze* shaking hands.

"Your husband? What has *he* got to do with it?" asked Fay. "He's dead, isn't he?"

Laurel took the breadboard in both hands and raised it up out of Fay's reach.

"Is that what you hit with? Is a moldy old breadboard the best you can find?"

Laurel held the board tightly. She supported it, above her head, but for a moment it seemed to be what supported her, a raft in the waters, to keep her from slipping down deep, where the others had gone before her.

From the parlor came a soft whirr, and noon struck.

Laurel slowly lowered the board and held it out level between the two of them.

"I'll tell you what: you just about made a fool of yourself," said Fay. "You were just before trying to hit me with that plank. But you couldn't have done it. You don't know the way to fight." She squinted up one eye. "I had a whole family to teach *me*."

But of course, Laurel saw, it was Fay who did not know how to fight. For Fay was without any powers of passion or imagination in herself and had no way to see it or reach it in the other person. Other people, inside their lives, might as well be invisible to her. To find them, she could only strike out those little fists at random, or spit from her little mouth. She could no more fight a feeling person than she could love him.

"I believe you underestimate everybody on earth," Laurel said.

She had been ready to hurt Fay. She had wanted to hurt her, and had known herself capable of doing it. But such is the strangeness of the mind, it had been the memory of the child Wendell that had prevented her.

"I don't know what you're making such a big fuss over. What do you see in that thing?" asked Fay.

"The whole story, Fay. The whole solid past," said Laurel.

"Whose story? Whose past? Not mine," said Fay.

"The past isn't a thing to me. I belong to the future, didn't you know that?"

And it occurred to Laurel that Fay might already have been faithless to her father's memory. "I know you aren't anything to the past," she said. "You can't do anything to it now." And neither am I; and neither can I, she thought, although it has been everything and done everything to me, everything for me. The past is no more open to help or hurt than was Father in his coffin. The past is like him, impervious, and can never be awakened. It is memory that is the somnambulist. It will come back in its wounds from across the world, like Phil, calling us by our names and demanding its rightful tears. It will never be impervious. The memory can be hurt, time and again—but in that may lie its final mercy. As long as it's vulnerable to the living moment, it lives for us, and while it lives, and while we are able, we can give it up its due.

From outside in the driveway came the sound of a car arriving and the bridesmaids' tattoo on the horn.

"Take it!" said Fay. "It'll give me one thing less to get rid of."

"Never mind," said Laurel, laying the breadboard down on the table where it belonged. "I think I can get along without that too." Memory lived not in initial possession but in the freed hands, pardoned and freed, and in the heart that can empty but fill again, in the patterns restored by dreams. Laurel passed Fay and went into the hall, took up her coat and handbag. Missouri came running along the porch in time to reach for her suitcase. Laurel pressed her quickly to her, sped down the steps and to the car where the bridesmaids were waiting, holding the door open for her and impatiently calling her name.

"There now," Tish said. "You'll make it by the skin of your teeth."

They flashed by the Courthouse, turned at the school. Miss Adele was out with her first-graders, grouped for a game in the yard. She waved. So did the children. The last thing Laurel saw, before they whirled into speed, was the twinkling of their hands, the many small and unknown hands, wishing her goodbye.

About the Author

One of America's most admired authors, Eudora Welty was born in Jackson, Mississippi. She was educated locally and at Mississippi State College for Women, the University of Wisconsin, and the Columbia University Graduate School of Business. She is the author of, among many other books, *The Robber Bridegroom, Delta Wedding, The Ponder Heart, The Eye of the Story,* and *Losing Battles*. She died in 2001.

VINTAGE INTERNATIONAL

VINTAGE INTERNATIONAL

Now at your bookstore or call toll-free to order: 1-800-733-3000
(credit cards only).